CAUGHT IN THE FLAMES

THE FIRST RESPONDERS SERIES BOOK 5

JEN TALTY

JUPITER PRESS

CAUGHT IN THE FLAMES

The first responders series book 5

USA Today Bestseller
JEN TALTY

Newsletter signup

"Deadly Secrets is the best of romance and suspense in one hot read!" *NYT Bestselling Author Jennifer Probst*

"A charming setting and a steamy couple heat up the pages in a suspenseful story I couldn't put down!" *NY Times and USA today Bestselling Author Donna Grant*

"Jen Talty's books will grab your attention and pull you into a world of relatable characters, strong personalities, humor, and believable storylines. You'll laugh, you'll cry, and you'll rush to get the next book she releases!" Natalie Ann USA Today Bestselling Author

"I positively loved *In Two Weeks*, and highly recommend it. The writing is wonderful, the story is fantastic, and the characters will keep you coming back for more. I can't wait to get my hands on future installments of the NYS Troopers series." *Long and Short Reviews*

"*In Two Weeks* hooks the reader from page one. This is a fast paced story where the development of the romance grabs you emotionally and the suspense keeps you sitting on the edge of your chair. Great characters, great writing, and a believable plot that can be a warning to all of us." *Desiree Holt, USA Today Bestseller*

"*Dark Water* delivers an engaging portrait of wounded hearts as the memorable characters take you on a healing journey of love. A mysterious death brings danger and intrigue into the drama, while sultry passions brew into a believable plot that melts the reader's heart. Jen Talty pens an entertaining romance that grips the heart as the colorful and dangerous story unfolds into a chilling ending." *Night Owl Reviews*

"This is not the typical love story, nor is it the typical mystery. The characters are well rounded and interesting." *You Gotta Read Reviews*

"Murder in Paradise Bay is a fast-paced romantic thriller with plenty of twists and turns to keep you guessing until the end. You won't want to miss this one..." *USA Today bestselling author Janice Maynard*

BOOK DESCRIPTION

Morgan Farren, a ranger in the Adirondacks, hasn't thought much about settling down. He likes his nice quiet life in the mountains where most of his interaction with people limited to those who enjoy the great outdoors as much as he does. However, when his sister shows up with her friend Izzy not only does he find himself questioning life away from civilization, he questions why he chose this path in the first place.

Senior Firefighter, Lizzy Cohen is the kind of woman who likes to party. If she's not out at a nightclub, she's not having a good time. And spending time in the great outdoors isn't her idea of blowing off steam. But when a sexy park ranger starts pointing out the constellations, she finds herself realizing there's more to life than Tequila.

*S*enior Firefighter Lizzy Cohen brushed the damp hair from her muddy face as she set her helmet on the bench in front of her locker. Resting her arm across the metal, she closed her eyes and leaned her forehead into her elbow.

She didn't dare take a deep breath. Not yet. It didn't matter that she was back inside Station House 29, where the air was clean, free of soot and thick, black smoke.

No demons in this building would come out of the woodwork and terrorize her. No memories from the past to torment her and remind her of who she really was and what that meant.

Only her mind could do that now, and no fucking way would she let that happen.

She stiffened her spine, blinked, and blew out a puff of air. All she needed was a hot shower and a good shot of tequila.

Or two.

Fuck. Make it a night to forget.

And who could blame her after the long day she'd had.

"Hey," Cade Nash, the captain of the house, said as he tapped on the locker room. "How are you holding up?"

God, she hated that damned question. Not to mention being sick and tired of it. Ever since her fucking boss found out who she was, he'd gotten all weird, especially when dead bodies were involved.

"I'm fine." She rounded her shoulders and wiggled her fingers.

Cade pointed to the second floor. "You know the rules, and I'm certainly not going to bend them for you."

"Did I ask you to?" For as long as she'd known Cade, which was about two years, he was known for being a hard-ass. He wanted his crew to follow the rules, and he didn't bend or break them often, but he was a fair man and cut his people slack when appropriate. However, in this situation, he wasn't going to let her walk out that door without following protocol.

Spending a few moments with the department shrink after a ten-car pileup when a chemical tractor-trailer overturned just outside of the village and six people were killed was not something Cade was going to let slide, and she couldn't blame the man, even if she thought it was overkill considering these things happened in her line of work.

"No. I'm just making sure you're not trying to duck out before speaking to Doctor Greene."

"I wouldn't dream of it." Of course, she'd tried it twice before. The first time she'd successfully escaped the building, only to be forced to stay at the station for a full day after she'd clocked out until the good doctor could make her way in to do the official interview. The second time, Lizzy got halfway to her car before Cade chased her down, threatening to suspend her for a week. That's when she realized Cade wasn't going to give her a break when it came to the shrink.

Ever.

"Right. And my wife can't stand it when I fall asleep on the sofa." Cade chuckled. "Go take a shower, and then I expect you in the conference room. Got it?"

"Yes, sir." She snagged her shower caddy and bag, then marched herself off toward the women's restroom.

"Lizzy," Cade called.

Standing in the doorway, she glanced over her shoulder. "Yes?"

"Fletcher and Spencer said you did good out there."

"Thank you, sir." She swallowed the guttural sob that caught in her throat. The accident wasn't anything like what happened years ago. Pulling a young girl from the wreckage and performing CPR, only to have her not make it, but it brought everything to the surface. Anytime anyone didn't survive, it reminded her of what she'd lost.

Worse.

How she'd lost it.

Cade nodded. "Are you sure you want to leave Station 29? Lake George?"

"This is the longest I've been at any station, and it feels like it's time to move on. I like change," she said. "It's my thing."

"After what Fletcher said about your instincts and what everyone says about you on the job, I don't want to see you go. You're good at what you do, and you fit in here. I've gone through a few firefighters

4

for various reasons, but when I find one that fits the vibe of my house, I want to do whatever it takes to keep them. What's it going to take?"

"I appreciate the vote of confidence, but my mind is made up."

He waved his hand over his head. "I will give you a glowing recommendation."

"Thank you." She made her way to the bathroom. She'd been to seven stations since she'd started her career. If she were any other firefighter, she'd make this her home. It had everything she was looking for in a house. Good men and women. A consistent rotation of teams and variations in shifts between twelve-, twenty-four-, and forty-eight-hour shifts. Not to mention the location. Lake George had to be the most beautiful place she'd ever been and even though she'd never really left the state of New York, she couldn't imagine that any other place on earth could compare.

She stood under the hot shower and let the water sting her skin, turning it pink. She didn't care about lathering up, though she did just to get the smell of gasoline out of her hair and to stall a few extra minutes. Talking to psychiatrists always made her nervous. They wanted her to share her feelings regarding her job's difficult aspects when she only wanted to forget about them. What she did for a living was hard enough and while the doctors were well meaning and only wanted to help, they failed to understand that when she left the station, she needed to leave her work behind. Taking it home with her was not only dangerous to her mental health, but it was detrimental to her performance.

Or at least that's the line of crap she fed herself.

Wrapping her body with the towel, she slipped from the stall, pausing as she stepped into the dressing area. "Hey, Emma."

"Hey, yourself." Emma Bryant was Spencer's younger sister. Spencer happened to be married to Echo, who just happened to be one of Lizzy's best friends since she moved to the area. Actually, Echo had been a friend to Lizzy when they'd been kids, but Echo knew her as someone else. Lizzy often wondered what any of these people would do if they ever found out she was actually Eliza Cohen, and they had known her thirteen years ago.

She suspected Echo would see it as a form of betrayal.

And rightfully so.

Lizzy was living a lie, but one she had to, especially when she'd moved to Lake George.

It would be hard to leave this station, but harder

to leave her friends. However, she'd done it once years ago; she could do it again. "I take it Cade sent you down here to ensure I didn't try to run."

"He did," Emma admitted. "But I wanted to find out if you would like to get a drink with me after this."

"Hell, yes," Lizzy said. "I was hoping someone would make that suggestion. Who all is going?"

"Mostly just me and my brother. Of course, Echo is meeting us there with half her family. Her brother, Morgan, is in town."

"When did he get into town?" Lizzy had a weird friendship if one could call it that, with Morgan, whom every woman in town with a pulse voted to be *the sexiest man alive.*

Lizzy would have to agree, and if he was interested in going out and having a good time, she might actually consider him short-term material. However, he was her friend's older brother, which would make things icky, and his idea of a good time was pointing out the constellations in the sky, while Lizzy preferred nightclubs, tequila, or dancing.

Which meant he wasn't Lizzy material.

Besides, Lizzy didn't *do* boyfriends. She did casual flings that started in a blaze of glory and fizzled out after a few months with little fanfare.

"I can't say no to Echo," Lizzy said as she fingered her wet hair. That must have been what Echo's text had been all about. Lizzy would have to make sure she responded as soon as she was done with the good doctor.

"Oh, but you could say no to me?"

Lizzy leaned closer to the mirror and puckered her lips. She didn't wear a ton of makeup, but she didn't enter a bar without the bare minimum, and tonight would be no different.

It wasn't about any of the men that might be there, though that was part of it. However, Lizzy always wanted to look her best for herself.

At least that was the storyline she played in her head, and there was no fucking way she was going to change it now. Her life worked for her and no shrink was going to change her mind.

"I could absolutely say no to you," Lizzy said with a laugh. She adored Emma, and while Station 29 had one of the closest ratios of men to women in all the station houses in Upstate New York, Emma still had to be her favorite female co-worker and probably her closest friend in the workplace.

No way would Lizzy ever let Emma and Spencer's older sister, Rochelle, who also worked as a firefighter, know that fun little fact. Rochelle was fun enough, but she could be judgmental at times.

"I'll remember that," Emma said. "I'm so glad Echo got a babysitter and even happier that my idiot brother agreed to go out. This will be their first time leaving the baby with a nonfamily member."

"It will be good for them." Lizzy tossed the last of her makeup back into her pouch. "I better get up there before Cade has my ass on a platter."

"I'll see you at the Mason Jug." Emma tapped the wall and turned on her heel, disappearing into the hallway.

Lizzy sucked in a deep breath. She did her best to blink away the demons. Therapists tended to bring them out when she preferred they stayed in the darkest corner of her mind. Of course, it was harder being in her hometown.

She entered the conference room and put on her best *I'm fine* smile. "Hello, Doctor Greene."

"Please. It's Becky." The doctor waved her hand to the chair at the end of the large table.

Lizzy had first met Becky a year ago after a similar tragedy, pushing Lizzy into a dark space. Since then, Lizzy had managed to keep her shit together and she didn't plan on having anything derail her current halfway decent mood, which she kept going by keeping a mental picture of the sexy Morgan in her mind. "It's good to see you again, though not under the circumstances."

"I'm glad I was able to get here today and not have to do these tomorrow." Becky leaned back and rested her hands on her lap. "How are you feeling?"

"A little shaken up." Lizzy knew the drill. She needed to give Becky enough emotion to show that she was indeed affected by what happened.

That was the easy part because Lizzy was slowly dying on the inside. The only way she survived the death and destruction surrounding her job was the hundreds of calls she went on that saved lives.

And the ability to push down the pain.

For the most part.

"That was a bad accident," Becky said.

"It sure was." No reason to lie or downplay reality. What happened today was horrific, and Lizzy really didn't want to relive it. She needed to put it where it belonged. In the past. Every tragic call she went on was part of her civic duty. She couldn't dwell on any one of them, so she had to put each of them in a box not to be reopened. "I'd say it was the worst accident I've ever been called to in my career."

"And how does that make you feel?"

That was the question she didn't know how to

answer truthfully. Her emotions were complicated, and she tried not to let any of them rise to the surface. When they did punch through her carefully crafted wall, they always came out backward. But she had to give Becky something. "Shitty," Lizzy said. "But it's my job and I knew that when I signed on, so I have to keep moving forward because the next time the siren rings, I have to be a hundred percent."

Becky uncrossed her legs, shifted, and recrossed them. "It sounds like you don't deal with your emotions."

"No. I do. I just can't do it here or while I'm on the job." Probably not the right response, but it was the best one she could come up with on the spot.

"So where and when do you deal with all the tragedies your job brings your way?"

"The same way many of my co-workers do." Lizzy leaned forward, placing her hands on the tabletop. "I often take out my frustrations on a punching bag. I will go for a run. I'll hang out with a group from the station. I'll do whatever it takes to make sure that the ugly part of the job doesn't linger too long. I know it's there. I accept it. But I hold on to those moments and those calls where I and those I work with helped someone. Saved someone. Even though today's accident was deadly, not everyone lost their life, and we were able to do some good." She tapped the center of her chest. "*That* I hold on to. And *that* keeps me sane. It's why I became a firefighter."

Becky opened her mouth, but Lizzy wasn't finished. "I came into this career out of tragedy. I was motivated to save lives because of the ones my parents took. I knew that I wouldn't be able to save everyone. That I would see more death in this career. I accept that. It doesn't make it any easier, but I do have to compartmentalize my emotions; otherwise, I'd never get through a single day, and I wouldn't be able to perform my job to the best of my ability, and I'm good at what I do." None of that was false, except she did leave out the massive amounts of drinking that would take place this evening to get her through to tomorrow.

And maybe it would take three or four nights before the images from the accident would stop blending into the memories from her past, but she'd get there.

She always did.

"You have a tough exterior, but you don't have to be strong all the time," Becky said. "Letting your feelings out. Being emotional isn't a sign of weakness."

"I never said it was." Lizzy let out a long breath. She had one breakdown, and her boss thought she was a loose cannon. "Look. I know you're just doing your job and I know my past is a red flag of some kind."

Becky raised her hand. "No. Not at all. As a matter of fact, you're not the first firefighter that has sat across from me who has suffered a loss that pushed them into this career path or who had parents who were criminals. It was those crimes your parents committed that helped you become a better person. I admire that. However, a year ago, you went into a dark place after a tough call."

"I was suffering from burnout. I hadn't had a vacation in a long time and was coming off a double shift. Any one of us could have had an emotional breakdown after that call." Lizzy swallowed. Hard. She'd pulled two adults and one kid from that blaze.

The adults survived.

The child did not.

"You know it was more than that," Becky said.

"I've dealt with it. I'm fine. Really."

Becky pushed her card across the table.

Lizzy laughed. "Cade is more than worried, isn't he?"

"He cares about his crew."

13

That was an understatement. Half the station was related to Cade, and the rest he treated as though they were either his children or his younger brothers and sisters. Cade proved to be the best captain she'd ever worked under, which is why she'd gone to him about the transfer instead of just doing it.

She'd also never allowed herself to get close to her team.

Until now.

And that was a problem.

Becky leaned back. "Cade told me you're looking for a new job at a different station."

"That wasn't for Cade to tell anyone." Lizzy bit down on her tongue. She'd gone to Cade out of respect and because she'd like to keep her job until she found another one, especially since she was looking out of state, and that often required her to do more training and certification, which she could do on her days off. Cade had no business going behind her back and telling Becky about her plans, and Lizzy had every intention of letting Cade know he'd crossed a line.

"You're right. It wasn't. However, he's concerned about you and thought that some things might be tied together, and I tend to agree."

"I don't see how me letting him know my plans to move last week have anything to do with what happened a couple of hours ago. I only told him I planned on leaving because I felt I owed it to him because of our working relationship and how close I've become to everyone here. Otherwise, I would have waited until I found a new job and given him the standard two weeks' notice, which is what most would have done in my situation." And this right here was why Lizzy needed to get the fuck out of small-town Lake George, New York. No matter how much she'd grown to like it, it wasn't the place for her. She couldn't breathe anymore. She had no idea why she thought this would be better than working in any other place.

"You're pulling a lot of hours, taking on double shifts, and when you can't get shifts here, you find them with security companies. This has become a pattern for you during the months leading up to the time of year your parents were arrested."

Lizzy blinked. "Are you serious right now? You're really going to go back to when I was fourteen years old, and my folks got pissed off and lit a few buildings on fire and the destruction they caused and what that might have done to me psychologically?"

Becky arched a brow. "That's the motivation for why you became a firefighter in the first place, and it's commendable." Becky raised her hand. "But as I said to you during our sessions in the past, there is a component of blame and guilt you're still holding on to."

Lizzy had enough. She was tired of this dialogue. It was like having a conversation with a toddler who never stopped asking why. "Of course there is. I accept that I have survivor's guilt when it comes to Karen. I know that I often wonder why I lived, and she didn't. I still shed a tear or two over it, especially when we hit the anniversary of her death. I think that's normal. But I've learned that no matter how hard I try, no matter how good I am at my job, I can't save everyone. And I understand that the firefighters and other first responders did everything they could the day that Karen died. I place no blame on them or have this weird idea that it should have been me and not her. I just wish that she didn't have to die, period."

"I believe you." Becky tapped her temple with a pencil. "Your mind knows that. But does your heart and soul?"

Oh, for fuck's sake. "Yes. It's hard some days to reconcile all of it, but I know in my heart of hearts that I'm here for a reason. The work I do day in and day out is in memory of Karen and her parents."

"But you have the added element that it was your—"

"I know. I get it. And today was tough. Maybe tougher for me than others. It did hit me hard, but I'm okay. Really. I am."

"I think we need to consider the fact that the fire last year and today's crash are both only fifteen miles from where you grew up, how that is affecting you, and why you're now talking about leaving the state."

She flattened her hands on the tabletop and sucked in a deep cleansing breath. This was another reason she needed to get the fuck out of Upstate New York.

Too fucking close to home.

Becky certainly got that right.

"I like to travel, and I want to see more of the country. I'm lucky I can do my job anywhere and most places are looking for good firefighters."

"You started out in Buffalo, moved to Rochester, then Syracuse, and—"

"Then I ended up in New York City, before Albany, and finally landing my ass in this station. I know where I've worked."

"I just find it fascinating that you've worked your

way across the state, moving closer to your hometown."

Lizzy shrugged. "I got to see the great state that I was born in. Now, it's time to move on. I have a list of states and cities I want to work in. Would you like to see those?"

"Actually, I would."

"It's extensive." No fucking way was Lizzy going to do a deep dive into her bucket list of places to go or why she planned on going there, but she needed to give Becky something. "But right now, I'm applying to houses in Charleston, South Carolina."

"That's a beautiful area."

"It is. I love history and I'm fascinated by Fort Sumner." Not entirely a lie.

"The thing is, Lizzy, I'm worried, as is your captain, that you've been trying to connect to your past, but it's gotten to be too much, and now you're running, as you do at every station house, you go to."

Lizzy folded her arms across her chest. "Have you gone to my former captains?"

"No," Becky said.

"I resent that you and Cade are conversing about me behind my back."

"We're not." Becky waved her finger. "We had one conversation and that was today. He doesn't want to lose you either to another station or to the demons that haunt you. He'll take it personally."

"Well, he's going to have to get over it. I can't stand the winters anymore. Snow sucks. I want some sunshine." Lizzy stood. "I appreciate your concern and the conversation. Can I go now?"

Becky nodded. "You know how to reach me."

Lizzy took the card and tucked it into her pocket. "Take care." She'd forget the card was there by the time she got home. Her pants would end up in the laundry basket, and the card would get washed.

And Becky's phone number would get lost.

Lizzy would then be free to go visit the city Karen had been born in and spend a little time helping the good people of Charleston.

2

*M*organ Farren sipped his beer from his perch at the end of the bar. The nightclub scene, even a low-key one like at the Mason Jug, which wasn't really a club but more of a local watering hole with the occasional band, wasn't his bag.

"You look miserable," Tristan, a New York state trooper and one of Morgan's good friends, said. "My wife had that look on her face when I first met her."

"And he married me anyway." Brooke slapped Tristan on the shoulder. "Of course, he was like a bad rash that didn't go away."

Morgan laughed. "You two and my family are about the only reason I leave my mountain and come down here at all." He raised his beer. "I hope your kids turn out better than you."

"I should have known I'd end up having twins." Brooke rubbed her belly. "And these two use my uterus as a punching bag."

"Do you know what you're having?" Morgan asked.

"Yeah. Two of my wife," Tristan said. "Strong-willed and feisty as all get out." He shook his head. "I'm in so much trouble."

Brooke leaned in and kissed Tristan's cheek. "But we don't know the sex. We just know they have my wicked and wild personality."

Morgan had known Tristan most of his life. Morgan was a year older, and growing up, he and Tristan traveled in different circles, but they'd always been friendly. It had been a horrible day when Tristan's twin sister had died.

A day Morgan would never forget.

"I'm going to enjoy watching the two of you become parents. It will be more amusing than Spencer and my baby sister." Morgan shook his head. He still couldn't believe that Echo and Spencer had finally tied the knot in a wedding that had been planned for someone else.

But if there were two people that belonged together, it was Spencer and Echo. Thank God his sister finally figured that out.

"I'm surprised Spencer is here after that crash today." Tristan handed his credit card to the bartender. "Or anyone else for that matter. It was bad."

"That goes for you too, honey," Brooke said.

"I came in for the cleanup. I wasn't there for the brunt of it." Tristan looped his arm around his wife.

"Echo pushed Spencer to come tonight," Morgan admitted. "So did his sister, Emma, who was there as well. My two little brothers were first on the scene. I think they are struggling with this one, but Spencer said they are handling themselves like true professionals, and Echo is right; they need to get out and about and go on with their lives. Letting this fester in their minds will only make their jobs harder as they go forward."

"I agree. This was the kind of crash that causes nightmares." Tristan let out a slow breath. "But I've learned that life has to go on."

"That it does." Morgan eyed his brother, Noah, who had his arm around some hot redhead that he'd just met the other day, while his two little brothers sat at the bar a few stools down, chatting up some young ladies Morgan recognized from the neighborhood.

Tristan signed his receipt and slipped his card into his wallet. "My buddy, Josh, and his wife are here. They got a table outside. We'll catch you later."

"Good to see you again," Morgan said.

"Come down from the mountain more often." Brooke gave him a big hug.

"I'll be down when you have those babies." He smiled. And he'd keep that promise, but then he'd turn around and head right back to his post. He could only stand civilization for so long. If he didn't think his mother would have a fit, he'd move to Alaska.

His mother had some weird idea that the oldest child needed to set an example for the rest of the family, and she worried if he went too far from home, then everyone else would leave.

She all but blamed him when Echo took off after college, even though she outwardly supported her daughter and her decision to be a traveling nurse.

However, his mother wanted her boys to settle down and get married, even more so now that Echo had done exactly that.

Well, Noah was starting to talk about being tired of playing the field, but Hugh and Troy? Not even close. Especially Troy.

And not because he was barely old enough to drink.

However, the matriarch wholeheartedly believed that none of her younger male children were even in serious relationships because Morgan hadn't had a girlfriend that his family knew of since college. Now that Echo was married and had produced the first grandchild, his mother was on a mission to get Morgan married.

To anyone.

He cringed, raising his beer to Echo and her friend Lizzy Cohen. It wasn't that he didn't want to spend time with his baby sis, or even Lizzy for that matter. He actually liked Lizzy.

Hell, if Lizzy weren't as wild as a mountain lion, he'd consider taking her to bed. He nearly choked on the thought. That's *why* he should consider making his move, but he didn't get involved with his sister's friends. He'd done that once and it didn't end well.

Besides, Lizzy was a party girl who preferred a drink with an umbrella while listening to loud music instead of the music of crickets under a blanket of stars.

He hopped off the barstool and hugged his sister. "Wow. That baby weight just melted right off you."

"Aren't you sweet," Echo said. "Mom told me you're leaving first thing in the morning?"

"We're heading into the summer months. It's my busy time." Morgan stretched out his arm. "Good to see you again, Lizzy."

"You too." Lizzy gripped his hand and shook. Hard.

"Seriously? That's no way to greet a gentleman." He lifted it to his lips gently kissed the backside, and winked.

Lizzy laughed. "You're so weird."

"You can say that again," Echo said. "Is my *gentlemanly* brother giving up that stool for me?"

"Absolutely. I'm even buying the first round."

"Did I hear that you're buying?" Spencer appeared. It seemed like he came out of nowhere.

"A round of drinks," Morgan corrected. "You're buying dinner." No sooner did the words slip through his lips than he realized what his sister had done. He cocked his head.

Echo smiled triumphantly.

Sneaky little girl. But it would keep his mother off his back for the evening.

"Who else from the Farren-Bryant family will be joining our table?" Lizzy asked.

"It's just us," Echo said. "And our table is ready."

"Interesting how that worked out." Lizzy took her long dark hair and tossed it over her shoulder. "I need a shot of tequila."

Spencer held up his phone. "It's the babysitter. We need to take this."

"We should go out to the parking lot," Echo said.

"It takes both of you to answer a call?" Lizzy twisted her hair. She was more girly-girl than the other firefighters who worked at the station, and that surprised Morgan. Not that it was a problem, because he could do high heels and a skirt, but Lizzy was badass, so it just seemed like a bit of a contradiction.

But Lizzy was a walking contradiction to begin with.

"If you don't have a child, you don't have an opinion," his sister said as she followed her husband out the front door.

"I might join you in a shot," Morgan said as he offered his arm. "I have a feeling this is going to be one of those nights."

"You mean like that last time your sister tried to fix us up?"

"No. I mean more like the time my mom got in on the action." He nodded toward his folks, who were chatting with Spencer's mother. "I have no idea why they think we're a good fit. We're worse than oil and water."

"Actually, we have no idea. We've never taken each other out for a test drive." Lizzy gave him a little hip check as they headed into one of the side rooms where, thankfully, it would be quieter than the main room, but that could end up working against him if Spencer's mother got in on the whole, *Morgan needs a good woman* discussion.

Morgan's father, in this particular scenario, would have his back for about five minutes. His brothers would absolutely stand up for him, and he suspected Lizzy would tell them all how she wasn't even remotely attracted to him, but other than that, he was on his own.

"Are you suggesting we give all these people something to talk about?" he said with a short laugh.

"Abso-fucking-lutely-*not*. That would be like me buying anything generic. Not going to happen."

"Ouch. That hurt." He pulled out one of the chairs at their table.

"Oh. And I'm your style?"

"Can you go more than a day without taking a shower?"

"I can, but why would I want to? Besides, I generally smell like a fire, so I like to eliminate that smell."

"You know, the smell of a campfire is pretty sexy," he said.

"You're not weird. You're bizarre." Lizzy leaned back. She always came off as strong and independent, but Morgan could see a darkness and perhaps a bit of sadness in her eyes. Of course, Morgan was a shitty reader of people and their inner secrets. He never trusted his first instincts, and his first of hers had been pretty bad.

But Lizzy had grown on him.

Though not as much as his mother would have liked.

"Are you serious about doing a shot with me? Because here comes our waiter." Izzy pointed to a young man heading in their direction.

"Sure. Why not." He wasn't much of a drinker, so he would need to make sure his next round was water, or he might be crawling home.

"Look at you taking a walk on the wild side." Lizzy ordered a round of shots for the entire table, along with a plate of appetizers, which he was insanely appreciative of since he hadn't had anything to eat since breakfast.

"So, what have you been up to these days? I think it's been a couple of months since I last saw you." Morgan wasn't much of a conversationalist, but he'd mastered the art of small talk, which came in handy in situations like these.

"I'm looking to move."

He arched a brow. "Really. Why?"

She shrugged. "It's time for a change. New York is boring. I'm thinking about the Carolinas."

"Have you already quit your job?"

"Nope." She shook her head. "I've asked Cade to keep it quiet until I can find something, and I'm going to have to do some recertification, so I want to be able to do that on my time off. I won't be leaving for a few months. Unless Cade forces me to leave sooner."

"He won't do that. If he didn't want you to stick around, he would have told you to consider the conversation your two-week notice."

The Nash family and the Farrens were intertwined, and while Cade was older than Morgan, he'd gotten to know the man since his brothers started working at Station 29. Cade was the kind of guy you wanted in your corner, but don't cross him if you want to survive long term.

"He's already asked me not to leave and told me he'd give me a glowing recommendation," she said.

The waiter returned with their drinks.

He lifted the shot. "Here's to you staying for the summer."

She cocked her head. "Why?"

"I think you should come up to my neck of the woods and escape all this noise. Let me show you how beautiful nature can be."

"Are you propositioning me?"

He tossed his head back and laughed. "Lizzy. Trust me. I know better."

"Good." She raised her glass. "But I'll make a deal with you. I'll go to your mountain if you come dancing one night with me." She wiggled her finger. "One night. And I know you'll be back for the birth of your friend's babies."

"You've got to come to me first."

"Deal."

He tapped the shot glass on the table before bringing it to his lips. He downed the clear liquid and pounded his chest. "Jesus. I forgot how harsh that shit was."

"Are you kidding? It's as smooth as butter."

Before he could respond, the waiter set down a platter with a plethora of pre-game food for them to enjoy.

"Do you think your sister and Spencer are coming back? Or is it part of some bigger plan to get the two of us alone?"

"They're in the building." Morgan raised his water glass toward the front of the restaurant. "But they seem to be stalling."

"In that case, I'm drinking your sister's shot." Lizzy reached across the table, snagged one of the shot glasses, and downed it in less than five seconds.

It amazed Morgan that she didn't even make a face or need a chaser.

"I might as well follow suit since I'm staying across the street and don't have to worry about driving home." He downed the horrible liquid in one swallow, but he needed to chug his water after, and he knew he had made the worst face known to man. He didn't do shots well when he was younger, and it didn't get better with age. "The last time I drank tequila, I had the worst hangover, and I hate to admit it, but I was throwing up all day."

"You're a lightweight." Lizzy laughed.

"That is a truth I won't try to deny." He leaned to

the side, eyeing his sister. "Damn it. She's prepping to leave."

"Seriously?"

Morgan nodded. "I can't tell if maybe Spencer is staying or not." He took out his cell.

Morgan: What the hell is going on?

Spencer: Our babysitter's dad just went to the hospital. And that's no bullshit.

Morgan: Shit. Sorry. What can I do?

Spencer: Not give your sister shit for leaving, and I'm going to go with her even though she wants me to stay.

Morgan: Just go. Tell Echo I'll stop by for breakfast.

Spencer: Thanks. She'll like that.

"So, are you going to fill me in?" Lizzy leaned forward, taking a potato skin and stuffing half of it in her mouth.

He waved to the waiter. "Can we get the bill and a couple of to-go boxes?"

"What the fuck?" Lizzy dropped the tasty appetizer on the table. "You're going to leave me here with all these people?"

"That's up to you." While he loved his family and enjoyed all the Bryants, this was not how he wanted to spend his evening. "I'm going to take these fun foods and go hang out on my parents' dock and watch the moon and stars dance over the lake. You are welcome to join me." He leaned forward. "I know my dad has some good tequila, though I will stick with beer."

"Suit yourself." She pushed back and stood. "I'll see you in the parking lot."

He laughed. Now, all he had to do was sneak out without anyone noticing.

3

_L_izzy gripped the side of the boat. "This was a fucking bad idea." Tequila and a boat being tossed about by waves could only lead to one thing.

Morgan took her by the hips and helped her to the dock. "Where things went wrong was when you decided to bring the bottle of hard liquor with us."

"Yeah. Remind me that I'm not as good at drinking as I think I am while we're standing on something that is moving."

"It's just the waves, and we're now on dry land, so it should be better." He held her steady, rubbing his strong hands up and down her arms. "Feeling better?"

"I could use some bread and water. Anything to

soak up the booze in my gut." Lizzy rested one hand on his shoulder, and she flattened the other on her stomach, hoping it would ease the sloshing in her gut. "I'm just glad we didn't go for a ride. I would have really lost my cookies and that is something I would not have wanted to share with you."

"Come on. There's a fully stocked fridge in the lower level of my folks' house." He looped his arm around her waist, practically hoisting her off the wooden planks. "Though you're really not that drunk."

"No. But between the swaying and the lack of food for the last couple of hours, I'm feeling it."

"I'm sure you are." He opened the sliding door to his parents' modest house on Lake George. She always loved coming to the Farren abode. His family was fun and welcoming. Their home was always filled with sweet scents like cinnamon and vanilla. His sister, Echo, always told her it was a safe place to land.

Lizzy could understand why.

And even though her brothers were all a little overbearing, they meant well.

"Where do you live? I mean, do you actually live in the mountains?"

He laughed, and she just wanted to curl up in his

arms and listen to the rumble in his throat. It was a deep sound, but not loud. Surprisingly sophisticated. Morgan was the kind of man you wanted to get to know because he was such a closed book. That thought made her want to burst out giggling like a silly schoolgirl.

She was the one who had a wall built up so high that not even a bulldozer could get in. Perhaps that's why she was so fascinated by Morgan. Neither one of them wanted to get close to people. They'd managed to spend a good two hours talking about music, television, and books. But not a single intimate thing about each other.

And she suspected he preferred to keep things like that as much as she did. Only now she wanted to know at least one thing that made Morgan Farren tick. And she was willing to give up something personal to get it.

"When I'm working, I stay at one of the ranger stations, but I do own a house in North Hudson. It's kind of in the middle of nowhere, surrounded by foliage, with no neighbors in sight, but I like it."

She plopped down on the big leather sofa and took the water bottle he offered. "So, why a ranger?"

And there was that glorious laugh again. It rolled

through her system like butter, melting over warm bread.

"Ever since I was a little boy, I couldn't decide if I wanted to be a firefighter or a cop, but a ranger provided me a good mix, so I went for it."

"You're neither."

"I'm both." He handed her a sandwich.

She brought it to her nose and sniffed.

Peanut butter.

Her stomach growled. She stuffed half of it into her mouth and groaned. "You're far from what I do."

"That's true. But I do have firefighting training, and if a forest fire breaks out on my turf, I'll be right next to you, working on containment."

"I'll give you that." She waggled her finger. "I bet police officers accuse you of being a rent-a-cop."

"Not the state troopers I know." Morgan made himself comfortable next to her on the couch.

"You still haven't answered my question."

"Do you want the standard answer? Or the *I've had just enough alcohol not to give a shit* answer."

"Oh, definitely the latter."

"All right, but you have to give me the real reason you became a firefighter." He tapped his water bottle against hers and grinned like he just won a hundred bucks.

"I suppose that's fair. But I expect an in-depth, detailed answer, and I get to ask questions."

He held up his hand. "We can each ask five, but that's it."

She nodded. "Start talking."

"You don't want to go first? I mean, ladies and all."

"Fuck, no. See, I ain't no lady."

He leaned closer. His hand landed on her thigh. His hot breath tickled her cheek. "I beg to differ."

The air in the room grew thick. It became hard to fill her lungs. Her eyelids fluttered as his lips glossed over hers in a warm but way too-short kiss.

"As I told you, my mom holds me as an example for my siblings." He brushed a strand of her hair behind her shoulder and fiddled with her earring.

It took all her energy not to straddle him and prove to him she wasn't a sweet girl.

"So, when it became apparent that all I was interested in was fires and guns, my mom did her best to push me into anything other than that. She even suggested professional football, which she swore no child of hers would ever become involved in."

"Were you any good?"

"I was recruited by three Division I schools, but I

had no desire to play past high school. However, I also didn't want to fight with my parents or make my mama cry. Not that she would actually try to guilt me out of following my dreams, but there was always that little dig. Or that look. Or she'd even say occasionally how I had to set the tone for my baby brothers."

"So, you became a ranger as a compromise?"

"Pretty much, only it didn't do any good. I have three firefighting little brothers, and my sister married one. Go figure." He shrugged. "However, it all worked out for the best. I would have gone crazy if I had become a cop or what you do."

"Why?"

"I don't like people that much." He released her jewelry and dropped his hand to the back of the sofa. "Let me rephrase that. I prefer to be alone and I know that firefighters become a family. So do cops. While I'm close to the other rangers I work with, we don't have that kind of closeness with each other. I get a lot of alone time and I like it."

"What is it about people that rub you the wrong way?" She tucked her feet up under her butt and leaned back on the armrest. A slight breeze blew in through the open screen door. The sound of a lone motorboat cutting through the water filled the night air. She wasn't used to this kind of quiet, but she was oddly enjoying it.

"Obviously, it's not everyone. I prefer being outdoors. I always have. I drove my parents nuts." He pointed to the lake. "There's a camp up on the other side of the lake, about five miles up the road. I begged them to send me for the entire summer and not just two weeks."

"But you live on the lake."

He nodded. "I know. That was their problem. But I couldn't do all the things that camp offered here. And then they started this wilderness program, and I was head over heels for it. One summer I spent fourteen days hiking the very mountain range I'm assigned to right now. I found that I'm at my best when I'm in the outdoors, being one with nature. Not cooped up in the city."

"Lake George is a far cry from a city."

"That's true. And I do like to come home and visit. But I get squirrelly if I stay too long." He reached out and tucked a piece of hair behind her ear. "You have one last question. You might want to make it good."

She smiled. "You're a man. I'm sure you have needs. What about sex? I mean, you're up there, mostly alone, and while I'm sure you handle taking care of yourself just fine, it's not the same thing."

He tossed his head back and burst out laughing. A full-out belly laugh. It was so hard he rolled off the sofa and landed on the floor with a thud. "I don't know why I'm shocked that you said that."

"Me neither. And I want an answer."

He leaned his shoulder against her leg. "My sexual needs are satisfied, and I'm not talking about my right or left hand, but." He raised his finger. "I'm not a player, nor am I a big relationship guy. Let's just say I know a few ladies."

"Ah, you're one of those guys."

"What does that mean?"

She swung her leg over his head and pulled him closer, giving him a shoulder and neck massage. She knew she shouldn't. It was a blatant invitation to something more, and considering they were in his parents' basement, that probably wasn't going to happen.

Nor should it.

Morgan was her best friend's brother. Not to mention, three of his brothers were her co-workers.

It could easily get icky real quick. And there was the question of her past.

"You have a list of lady booty call girls."

"Oh. I don't think my female friends would like you calling them that. They certainly have more class."

Without thinking, Lizzy ran her fingers through Morgan's hair, curling them through the ends before rubbing the top of his neck. "If you're seeing them, I'm sure they do. But don't they mind sharing you?"

"That's six questions."

"I'll answer an extra one when it's my turn."

"I can't believe I'm going to tell you this." He dropped his head, leaning forward, giving her better access.

"You don't have to if you don't want to."

He twisted his body, glancing over his shoulder and catching her gaze. "I said I'd be honest. Will you do the same?"

"Yes." She'd lost her fucking mind. Not because she agreed, but because she knew she'd tell him the truth, and she had no idea why she felt so compelled to do so.

"I haven't had what anyone would call a conventional relationship in years." He shook his head. "Hell, I haven't had a relationship since college. The couple of women I know understand I'm not interested in anything, and neither are they. We use each other, but we have enormous amount of respect for one another. This might sound weird, but I never let them overlap. I kind of have a summer thing and a winter thing, but honestly, the summer girl ended because she met someone, and I would never get in the way of that."

"I can't decide if that's the sweetest thing I've ever heard or the most pathetic."

"It's both." He dropped his arm over her legs. "Your turn for some honesty."

"Where's the fucking tequila?"

"On the boat."

"Of course it is," she said with a slight laugh. "What was it that you wanted to know?"

"Seriously?" He climbed up on the sofa, pulling her between his legs. "You don't get to start by asking me a question."

"Fine." She rested her head against his strong frame, curling her knees to her chest, wishing she could fight the pull to be in his arms. She let out a long breath and decided to try to relax for once in her life.

If she ever had to describe the definition of an oxymoron in terms of a person, it would be Morgan. He might be introverted and a bit odd, but he was also intelligent, kind, sweet, and insanely adorable.

"I have no idea where to begin," she said. "I really

don't, so it would be easier if you asked me or told me what you wanted to know."

"You can't use that as a ploy to get me to use my first question."

"Aren't you the smart one." She snuggled deeper into his embrace. There was no way this ended in anything but a kiss good night before she stumbled to her rental. "You have to promise me you won't tell Echo. I don't think she knows any of this."

"You have my word."

"I mean it. The only one that I know of who has a clue is Cade, and that's only because he had an up-close and personal look at my childhood profile when something happened at work."

He pressed his lips on her temple. "Whatever you tell me, I will never breathe a word of it to anyone. I promise. You can count on that."

"It surprises me that very few people haven't put my name with my parents' names, especially in Lake George."

"Why, who are your parents?"

"Question number one." She raised her finger. "Jacob and Hannah Cohen. They set three fires. Two to car dealerships owned by their bosses and one to—"

"Ross and Monica Lands' home, killing their only daughter, Karen."

Lizzy swallowed. Tears formed in her eyes. Never in a million years did she believe this game would become this emotional this quickly.

She either needed it to end.

Or she needed a stiff drink.

"I can't believe you figured that out so quickly," she said.

"Cohen is a common name, but not when you put it with Jacob, Hannah, and fires."

"I should have changed my name."

"Why didn't you?"

Lizzy held up two fingers, indicating how many questions he'd used. Not so much for him, but because she needed to be done with this entire conversation. "Mostly because back then, I went by Eliza, not Lizzy. And when people ask me about my parents, I flat-out lie." Oddly, not many people asked her about her childhood. "But going back to why I became a firefighter, I was the only survivor—"

"I know. Spencer's father is the fire marshal. Before that, he was a firefighter in the same station that you're working at right now, and he was there that day. As a matter of fact, he was the one who pulled you from that fire. He talks about it a lot. I'm sure Spencer and Echo know, and out of respect, they aren't saying anything."

"Well, fuck." That was a big pill to swallow. If that were indeed true, there were a shit ton of other people that knew exactly who she was and weren't saying a damn fucking word.

Kudos to them.

She might have to thank each and every single one for their kindness, and that thought pissed her off just as much as the fact that people knew her shame.

"Can you be sure your sister knows? Because if she does, I can't believe she doesn't hate me."

"No. But that fire really shook up Spencer's dad. And my parents remember it like it was yesterday. They were friends with the Lands."

"I know. I recall that fact well."

"Oh, shit," Morgan said. "I forgot you were sort of friends with my sister through Karen."

"Karen and I are a year older than Echo, but we all went to the same school, and Echo was always a grade ahead in math."

"Yeah. She's the smart one in the family, that's for sure. Used to drive Spencer crazy. He had to study twice as hard to get good grades and Echo barely had to study."

Lizzy wrapped her arms around Morgan's shoulders. "She's going to be super pissed."

"Not if she already knows. Besides, my sister stopped holding grudges when she and Spencer got back together." He kissed the top of her head. "So, I think I understand why you became a firefighter. I mean, it's a pretty common theme when someone loses a person they care about to a fire."

"I'm not sure if it was Karen's death that put that desire in me or my parents' brand of murder."

Morgan hugged her tight. "I can't imagine what it's been like for you. I can't even wrap my brain around it."

When people did make the connection, they either took two steps back, as if she had some weird contagious disease, or they stared at her with pity in their eyes.

Morgan did neither.

Instead, he accepted he hadn't a clue as to what it would be like to be her. That was a refreshing concept.

"It's sometimes still surreal," she said, closing her eyes. Memories of her childhood flooded her mind. For years, she blocked even the best of her past from reminding her of her family life. She didn't want to feel the warmth and love that her parents once gave her because they so easily took it away with a single light of a match.

And they did not even seem to care.

"You have four more questions," she said, needing to break up the trip down memory lane. She hated any good feelings she had toward her parents. It didn't matter that they were good people up until they weren't. They had destroyed so many lives. They didn't deserve any kindness.

Not even in the form of a thought.

"We don't have to play—"

"You wanted to know more, and it's only fair. Besides, I stick to the deals I make."

"All right." He brushed her hair to the side. "You were in eighth grade when it happened. I remember watching some of the trial on television. They never showed you."

"Is there a question in there somewhere?"

"We all wondered where you went. Did you go to foster care?"

"No. My mom's half-sister, who lives in Buffalo, took me in. I lived there until I was twenty."

"Echo told me that you moved around a lot. Why?"

"Do you want my version of the reason or Cade's and the department shrink's?"

"Both."

Lizzy laughed. "They believe I've been working my way closer to home. And I think maybe they were right. I needed to come back here to know that I could and survive. Now that I have, it's time to do what I've always wanted, and that's to see more of the country. I can do that with my job."

"You sound like my sister with her traveling nurse thing, which is funny because Spencer wouldn't leave because of being a firefighter."

"I get that. It's not easy to leave the state. It requires some work on my part, but it can be done."

"People think I'm hiding in the mountains from civilization. Do you think you're running from forming connections?"

"Now you sound like Becky, the psychiatrist." Lizzy shrugged. "Does it really matter if I am or if I'm not? I mean, whatever my motivations, both consciously and subconsciously, they are immaterial as long as I'm above water and feel good about what I'm doing." She pushed to a sitting position and faced him. "I'm not an unhappy person."

"I never said you were." He arched his brow. "I get the same thing, so I'm not judging. I'm just asking."

"Speaking of which, you have two left."

"Are you still renting Spencer's old place down the street?"

"I am, but what does that have to do with our little game?" Her heart beat a little faster. Heat inched across her skin like water cascading from the showerhead.

"I'm choosing to use my questions on something else." He leaned closer and licked his lips. "I probably shouldn't even go down this road, and you might tell me to take a hike, but I think we can both agree that the last few times we've seen each other, there's been an attraction."

"What are you asking me?"

"Shall we take this back to your place?"

She palmed his cheek. "Why, Morgan Farren, are you propositioning me?"

"I'm working on it." He pressed his mouth over hers while his fingers curled around the back of her neck, massaging gently.

His kiss was tender but passionate. It wasn't over the top or harsh, but as he slipped his tongue between her lips, her toes flexed. She wanted to lose control in his arms and forget about everything for one night.

"Let's go," she whispered. "But this is just—"

"I understand. And before we go any further, I

want you to know I don't go to bed with just anyone."

"Neither do I. Truth be told, I'm a bit like you. No one overlaps. For right now, it's just you, and I know that come the crack of dawn, you're going back to your mountain."

He ran his thumb under her cheek. "I know you and I bicker most of the time, but I've always liked you, and I've had a secret crush on you."

"Right back at you." She jumped up from the sofa. She'd had enough talk. Time to get the party started. "I'll race you back to my place." With that, she was out the door. She could hear his feet hitting the ground only one pace behind her.

Something told her this night would be one of those nights that will forever be ingrained in her brain.

4

*M*organ couldn't blame this decision on booze. He hadn't had a drink in hours, and his faculties were completely intact. And using the fact he hadn't had sex in six months would be the absolute lamest excuse he could possibly come up with.

He leaned against her bedroom door, staring at her as the moonlight filtered in through the window, catching her hair and showing off her soft highlights. She ran her fingers through the long strands, fiddling with the ends right in front of her breasts.

"Either you're having second thoughts, or you really like the view."

"Both." He inched closer. "But I'd regret it if I left."

Her bright smile sent a warm shiver across his body. His fingers itched to touch her bare skin.

"Do you want to hear something funny?" She pulled her shirt over her head. Her hair bounced as it followed the fabric and then fell to her shoulders, cascading over her light-blue lacy bra.

The color matched her eyes.

"Sure." He wrapped his arms around her waist, flattening his palms over the small of her back.

"While your family has been trying to fix us up, and I've been saying no way each time, I bet a friend of mine from the last station house I was at that you and I would hook up at least once before I moved on."

"Does this mean when I come down from my mountain, there might be a chance I can sneak in your window at night?"

She slipped her hands under his shirt and yanked, sending it flying across the room. "On one condition."

He arched a brow as her hands glided over his skin.

She pressed her lips on his chest. "Your family can never find out."

"I have no problem with that because if they did, my mother would have us married in five minutes." He threaded his fingers through her long hair, gently pushing one of the straps of her bra off her shoulder.

"God save us both."

He chuckled. "Since we're keeping this— whatever this is—from Echo and the rest of the clan, I think it goes without saying...whoa."

She reached inside the front of his jeans, undoing the button and sliding the zipper down. "Since it goes without saying, don't say it." She dotted his abs with sweet kisses. Her tongue darted from between her plump lips as she continued lower and lower.

He watched as she removed the rest of his clothing and seamlessly took him into her mouth. Pooling her hair on top of her head, he did his best to remain in control as she gave him the kind of pleasure he'd imagined for months. If he'd been honest with himself, she'd been all he could think about when he allowed his mind to drift after work. And his heart beat a little faster every time he drove from North Hudson back to his family home since Lizzy had moved to the area.

He swallowed a guttural groan as she swirled her tongue over the tip, squeezing his shaft and blinking her eyes open. She practically smiled at him.

"Come here." Gently, he tugged.

She stood before him, slowly removing her bra, letting it dangle on her fingertips before dropping it to the floor.

He growled as she rolled her slacks over her hips. "You're beautiful."

"You're pretty incredible yourself."

There was nothing sexier than a woman with her hair over her breasts, and her hair covered them perfectly, letting her nipples poke through the strands. Any woman he'd ever been with he had desired with a great deal of passion. He never went to bed with someone where the sparks didn't fly.

Not only that, he liked his women to be smart.

Lizzy was the total package.

"You're a dangerous woman." He yanked back the bed covers and heaved her to his chest. Their lips locked in a fast-paced dance that had no chance of moving into slow motion anytime soon.

His hands roamed her toned body. He lifted her off the floor and set her on the edge of the bed. He kissed her neck and moved down to her breasts, sucking her nipple into his mouth while his fingers slipped between her legs.

She ran her hands through his hair, clutching tightly. Her breath became ragged.

Pushing her back, he traced a path down her belly with his tongue. He glanced up, catching her gaze.

His breath hitched.

He'd never met anyone like Lizzy before. She had a unique personality that some might consider harsh, but it was one of the things that attracted him to her in the first place.

It was also a big reason he'd kept her at a safe distance for so long.

Irresistible was about the only way to describe Lizzy.

She opened her legs a little wider and coaxed his head closer. "Please," she whispered.

His pulse kicked up. He lowered his head and licked his lips. He pressed his finger against her hard nub and was rewarded with a soft moan.

She tasted like a combination of watermelon and honey. Her heels dug into his back while he worked with his mouth and fingers. He wanted to find the perfect combination that would make her lose all control, and he didn't have to try too hard. Her legs slammed into the sides of his face. She pushed to a sitting position and cried out his name.

God, he could listen to the sound of her voice all day long.

More importantly, he wanted to feel her body convulse over and over again.

She fell back on the bed. "Morgan," she whispered. "Oh, my God." She clutched her breasts, which heaved up and down with every heavy breath. "I don't think I've ever come that fast or that hard in my entire life."

"I hope that's a good thing because in a guy's world, fast isn't something we strive for."

She laughed. "It's fantastic, and the best part is I can do that again. If it were you, you'd be done."

"My recovery time is probably a good hour."

"Sucks to be a man."

"Oh, I beg to differ." He propped himself up on an elbow and ran his index finger around the edges of her nipple. It tightened and puckered under his touch. "I need to ask about birth control, though I do have a condom in my wallet."

"I hate those things."

"Can't say they are my favorite, but they serve a few purposes."

She pushed him to his back and straddled him. "I'm on the pill, and I'm clean."

"I am too." He gripped her hips. "Clean that is. I mean, I'd worry that taking the pill might mess with my hormones."

She leaned over and brushed her lips over his. "You're funny."

"I have my moments." He stared deep into her eyes as he thrust himself inside her in one powerful stroke.

Arching, she tossed her head back and rocked, grinding against him.

There was no slow buildup. No getting to know what the other needed or what each other's bodies wanted because they already knew.

However, this would be a test of his ability to maintain control. He just hoped he could hold out long enough to ensure her another orgasm. Perhaps another position might bode better for him, but the moment he tried, she stopped him, and who was he to deny her the kind of pleasure she demanded.

He reached up and brushed her thick, soft hair over her shoulders and cupped her round breasts. They were lost in the palm of his hands. He squeezed and molded them, occasionally letting his thumbs scrape across her hard nipples. He concentrated on his hands and her moans as she rocked back and forth, taking exactly what she needed.

As she moved faster, grinding harder, he slowly moved his hands over her tight stomach. He gripped her hips, taking some control over the movement. Reaching between them, he found her swollen nub.

"Oh, Morgan, yes," she said with a moan. She leaned forward, pressing her hands on his chest, intently locking gazes. She tightened around him as her body convulsed. "Morgan." Her climax wrapped around him like a python squeezing its prey, only it was the most amazing sensation he'd ever experienced.

His toes curled as he flipped her to her back, unable to control himself any longer. He thrust into her with such need it frightened him.

She wrapped her legs around his waist and stared so deep into his eyes that he thought he might get lost forever.

And he would be okay with that.

He shivered and paused for a moment. He tried to fill his lungs, but he couldn't.

Lizzy had stolen his breath, and in this small sliver of time, he feared she might have done the impossible and stolen his heart.

"What's wrong?" she whispered.

"Nothing," he said. "I just wanted to admire your beauty for a second."

She smiled. "That's so weird and sweet at the

same time." She squeezed his ass, encouraging him to finish what they started.

He didn't hesitate, taking her mouth, swirling his tongue in a wild dance while they ground against each other. His climax exploded only seconds later as she dug her heels into the back of his knees and cried out his name one last time.

Kissing her cheek, neck, and shoulder, he eased his weight on top of her and slowly tried to catch his breath.

And clear his mind of all the dangerous ideas that were beginning to form.

After a long while, he rolled to the side and pulled the covers over their bodies. He looped his arm around her, tucking her head to his chest so he could run his fingers through her long hair. He stared out the window at the moon and the stars casting their soft white lights over the dark lake below. A slight breeze rippled across the water. In a couple of hours, the sun would take over the night sky, and Morgan would return to where he was most comfortable.

He kissed Lizzy's temple.

No woman ever fit like she did. No lady ever made him question staying a second day. Sure, he cared about every person he'd ever dated. He didn't just hop into bed with anyone. And right now, he only wanted to share it with Lizzy.

"I can feel you thinking." She pressed her lips against his chest.

He chuckled, trying to make light of his thoughts. "I was just thinking about how much it was going to suck to sneak back into my parents' house at my age."

She laughed. "Yeah. We don't need you doing the walk of shame."

He let out a long sigh. "That means I should probably leave before I get too comfortable and fall asleep." That was the last thing he wanted to do, but it was the lesser of two evils because dealing with his mother if she found out would be hell.

"When do you think you will be back in town?"

He smiled. "Unless Tristan's wife has her babies sooner, about three weeks."

"When is she due?"

"Six weeks, but she's having twins, so she'll deliver early."

"What's in three weeks?" Lizzy asked.

Fuck. Lizzy's surprise birthday party was in three weeks. He might have just spilled the beans. Of course, he hadn't planned on returning for it, but things had changed.

"A buddy of mine asked me to give him a hand with a project." Now, he just had to come up with a friend and something that would require his help.

"That's nice of you."

"I had a few days off, and my mom has been bitching I don't come home enough. She still likes to have family dinners on a regular basis."

"I've been to a few of those. Your little brothers are hysterical." She pushed to a sitting position, wrapping herself in the sheet. "You're not going to tell anyone that I'm Eliza, are you?"

He shook his head. "But be prepared for the fact they already know."

She nodded.

"There is no shame in being you." He reached up and tucked her hair behind her ear. "You're not your parents."

"Oh. Trust me. I know that."

"Why don't you want people to know? Especially my sister?"

"When I first came here, I figured everyone would just know. Most people do a little double take when they look at me and hear my name. But no one has ever said anything. I act like I don't know anyone. I know I look a little different. I was a very late bloomer, so I barely even had boobs when I left."

"I like the way your breasts grew very much."

She laughed. "Even my hair color is different, but I just figured someone would recognize me, but no one did until Cade found out from the shrink, but he's told no one."

"And he won't. Not unless he has to for some strange reason. But if the department psychiatrist knows, and it's in your record, Spencer's father knows too. But I still don't understand why."

"I'm not sure I do either anymore other than I don't want to be Eliza, daughter to convicted arsonists and murderers. I just want to be Lizzy, the firefighter."

He sat up and stared into her blue eyes. "This might get me kicked out of bed, but ever since you moved here, you've kept people at a safe distance. Even my sister."

She arched a brow. "How would you know? We've been around each other maybe six times."

"Because during every single one of those times, I've wanted to take you to bed," he admitted. "However, you use partying as a form of defense. As a way to protect yourself from getting close to people. And you drink entirely too much."

She narrowed her eyes. "I don't need your

judgment, especially when you hide alone on a mountain, avoiding close personal contact."

Whatever Lizzy knew about his life or didn't know was immaterial. All she wanted to do was deflect, and he completely understood. If the tables were turned, he'd do the same thing because she was spot-on. But he wasn't about to admit that.

"I'm really not judging you."

"It certainly feels that way," she said, pulling the covers tighter around her body.

"I'm sorry. I didn't mean for it to come out that way. I'm just saying that maybe those things are connected. That maybe you're pushing people away and using the partying to avoid letting the person you've become heal the little girl you once were."

"What are we now, a fucking shrink?" She jumped off the bed and found a long shirt. "Why the hell did you have to go and ruin a perfectly good night?"

He ran a hand through his hair. Yeah. His timing was pretty fucked up, that's for sure. "Lizzy, I—"

"Save it," she said. "It's late. Or it's early. You've got to go over to Echo's in a few hours and then drive up to the Dix Range. You should probably go."

He hiked up his pants and closed the gap. He

took her in his arms, and thankfully, she did not push him away. "I'll see you in a couple of weeks."

She rested her hands on his shoulders and kissed him quickly before stepping back.

Well, he'd bet the condom he had in his wallet she wouldn't be inviting him into her bed the next time they crossed paths. "Good night, Lizzy."

"Walk home safely," she said.

And with that, he gathered the rest of his things and made his way across the lakefront yards to his childhood home, where he found his father sitting on the back deck with a mug.

Mother fucker.

"Hello, son," he said.

"Dad." Morgan tossed his shoes by the door and pulled his shirt over his head. "What are you doing up?"

"It's five thirty in the morning. I'm almost always up this early."

Morgan glanced at his Apple Watch.

Dead.

Shit. He had no idea it was that early.

"The real question is: Where have you been all night? And don't try to say you went for a walk or some such bullshit because your mother is awake, and when she saw your bedroom door open, she, of course, went to get the sheets, and guess what she found?"

"A made bed," Morgan said, knowing his father wasn't going to sugarcoat it. He hadn't while Morgan had been growing up; why would he start now that he was thirty-one? "I hope she's not too worried."

"She was freaking out about five minutes ago. Came out here, and that's when she saw you walking across the yards. She let out a sigh of relief and was inside making another pot of coffee."

"Wonderful."

"I think that modular home should be named the hookup house." His father raised his mug.

Morgan's cheeks flushed just like they had when he'd been seventeen years old, and he got caught with his hand up a girl's shirt on the boat. "That's really not funny, Dad."

"It started with Tristen and his wife. Then your sister and Spencer were doing the—"

"Don't even say it. That's really gross coming from you."

"They're married. With a kid. It's not like I don't know they're having sex."

Morgan shook his head. "At least I'm not having this conversation with Mom."

"Oh. She's pulling out the wedding magazines."

"Fuck," Morgan mumbled. "She can't say a word to Lizzy. Not a single word. She just can't."

"She won't. I'll make sure of it. But why? Please don't tell me you took advantage of a drunk girl?"

"Jesus, Dad. You know me better than that. Of course not." Morgan rubbed the back of his neck. He couldn't break Lizzy's confidence. Not even to his father. That wouldn't be fair. "Do I really have to answer that question? I mean, I spend one night with a lady, and Mom goes all batshit crazy and has me walking down the aisle. Not only does it make me want to run right back to my mountain, as everyone calls it, but it scares away anyone I've ever brought around."

"You haven't brought a girl home since Randi."

God, he hated hearing that woman's name for a plethora of reasons, but mostly because she'd nearly destroyed him, and it had taken him a long time to pick up the pieces of his life. "There hasn't been anyone worth bringing home."

"And why is that? Besides, it's hard to find someone when you spend all your time alone," his father said with a heavy dose of sarcasm and a spoonful of disappointment.

"Do you want the truth? Because you and Mom aren't going to like it."

"I always want that from you, son."

"I like being alone. Sharing my life with someone takes the kind of work I'm unwilling to do. And after Randi, I don't want to risk it."

"Not every woman is a Randi," his father said.

"Oh. I know that. I can look around me and see hundreds of women who are nothing like that"—he wanted to say bitch but would refrain—"person. I mean Mom, Echo, Brooke, Jared's wife, and the list goes on and on and on. But that's not the point. Randi isn't why I don't want to be in a committed relationship. What you all fail to understand is that it wasn't just Randi's fault our relationship crashed and burned. As a matter of fact, I played a bigger role in that than she did."

"And how is that?" His mother's voice echoed in the still morning air. She set a pot of coffee and two mugs on the table and perched herself on one of the other chairs. "Please, continue."

Morgan took a few moments to fill his cup. He really didn't want to have this conversation with his dad, even less so with his mother, but he was cornered. There was no way out, and he had too much respect for his folks to storm off.

"Randi wanted to get married. She wanted kids. She wanted the whole ball of wax, and I wanted to wait. She pushed, and she pushed, and she pushed. And I kept saying after college we'd talk about it, but she wouldn't stop. We were only twenty-one. So, when we graduated, she basically told me if I went to ranger school we were done. I said fine, we're done. No one was going to take my dreams away from me."

"And no one should," his mother said. "But there was more to your breakup than that."

He nodded. "I never wanted to burden you with the gritty details."

"Well, burden us now." His mother reached out and squeezed his shoulder. "It's what we're here for."

He patted her hand. "Looking back, I'm not sure I loved Randi like you're supposed to, but the big thing for me was I thought we were too young, and I didn't want to settle down and have kids right away. And she didn't want to move to the middle of nowhere. So, we were still in the same constant battle, and I once again broke up with her. It just wasn't worth all the fighting. We were both miserable."

"She wasn't right for you," his father said.

Morgan wouldn't argue that point. "About two

weeks after I ended it, she came to me and told me she was pregnant."

The sound of ceramic hitting wood and shattering into a million pieces made him jump.

"Oh, crap," his mother said, pushing her chair back.

"Don't move, dear." His father stood.

"Everyone, sit down. This mess can wait. I want to hear the rest of this first." His mother tucked her feet up under her butt. "What happened to the baby?" she asked with wide eyes.

"There was never a baby. She lied. But I didn't find out until I was standing in city hall about to marry her."

His mother's face turned white. Her jaw slacked open.

"Mom? Are you okay?" He curled his fingers around her forearm.

She shrugged it off. "No. I'm not. First, how did you find out she wasn't pregnant?"

"We needed a pen, and I went in her purse to get one and found tampons. What does a pregnant lady need with those? I confronted her and then demanded proof and said I wouldn't marry her until I had that in my hands. The proof never came."

The color slowly returned to his mother's face, making him feel a little better.

"What else do you want to know?" he asked.

"I think that answered my questions," his mother said. "I'm sorry you had to go through that alone. But I'm also angry as hell that you didn't come to us, especially since you were going to marry her."

"I didn't want to, which is why I didn't want you there. It felt wrong to begin with. It would have felt even more so if I had let you in." He stood, stepping around the broken mug. He leaned over his mother and hugged her tight. "I'm sorry. I didn't mean to keep any of that from you except that I was ashamed of what I'd let happen. But none of that is why I don't want to get married. However, that experience solidified the fact I love my life. I'm so lucky I get to have a career that satisfies me and I'm not lonely or anything. So, I wish you'd stop worrying about me."

His mother cupped his cheeks. "I will never stop worrying about my children. Ever. But I also know my kids better than they know themselves, and you, my son, have it bad for Lizzy. Now that you've spent the night with her, I suspect it will be hard for you to let her go, and unfortunately, you're going to find out what it's like to be lonely."

5

*L*izzy stared at the television. Her heart beat so fast she thought it might jump right out of her chest. Perspiration beaded across her forehead. She always knew it was possible but never thought the first parole hearing could happen so soon.

Or while she was living in the area.

But sure as shit, in three weeks, her parents would go before the parole board and ask to be released early.

On her goddamned birthday.

Fuck.

How they even got away with a third-degree murder conviction still haunted Lizzy to this day. Granted, the fires set to the dealerships were during nonbusiness hours. No one was in those buildings. And no one was hurt.

But the house?

They had to have known that the Lands were home. Or could have been home. Their *intent* had to have been to kill them, but it couldn't be proven, and they swore up and down their only motivation had been to destroy their property and take away their livelihood as they'd done to them.

Considering her parents were about to lose their home, and they'd lost their jobs, the jury bought it hook, line, and sinker.

And they were given a sixteen-year sentence.

Thirteen years in, they were up for parole.

Fuck. Fuck. Fuck.

Lizzy's phone buzzed.

Cade.

"Hello," she said.

"I just saw the news. How are you holding up?"

"I'm fine," she said. "Pissed at the system, but fine."

"Are you going to the hearing?"

She swallowed. "I don't know."

"If you decide you want to, I'll go with you. For moral support."

A single tear scorched a hot path down her

cheek. "I appreciate that. But I'm thinking more along the lines of transferring sooner. Like before the hearing." As if that were actually possible.

"Lizzy, don't. Running isn't the answer."

"I'm not running." She pointed the remote at the television and clicked the off button. "I'm living my life, and I've been trying to do it free of my parents' crimes." She made her way from the family room to the kitchen, which took all of ten steps, and pulled down a bottle of tequila. She checked the time.

It was four forty-five in the afternoon.

Well, it was five o'clock somewhere.

She poured three fingers into a small glass and sat down at the kitchen table.

"Moving back to Lake George says otherwise." Cade had a valid point.

One she needed to take a solid look at because moving around the state, seeing different cities was one thing.

Coming back to the one event that changed her world forever was something entirely different.

Of course, she stayed longer than she'd originally planned simply because she'd decided being in her hometown had little to no effect on her when, in reality, it had a hold on her soul and her heart. She hadn't realized how much so until the accident the other day.

And then there was Morgan.

It had been almost a week since she'd seen him, and while they'd texted a few times, she still didn't feel good about how they'd left things.

"Let me ask you something, Cade." She lifted the glass and swirled it around. Ever since Morgan had made the comment about her drinking and party girl mantra, associating it back to keeping people at a distance and avoiding things in general, she'd been trying to keep the alcohol consumption to a minimum.

But finding out her parents could be getting out of prison? Well, that was cause for a little numbness.

"If you were me, would you go to the hearings?"

"I have no idea," Cade said. "My first initial thought is hell yes. And I'd want to speak as well. But I'm not you and to be honest, I'm struggling to put myself in your shoes. However, I will say this. You made your way across this state and landed back here for a reason. Don't just up and leave. You have people here who care about you and Station 29 is your home."

She squeezed her eyes closed. A couple more

tears rolled down her cheeks. She swiped at her face. "I appreciate you saying that."

"Those aren't empty words. I mean them," Cade said. "I can't believe I'm even going to suggest this because I'm terrified I'll lose you, but maybe you need to take a week off of work. Clear your head. Get some perspective."

She set the glass down and pushed it away. "I think you might be right about that, and I'm going to take you up on it."

"All right. I can make that work in a week or two, but you must promise me two things."

"I'm afraid to ask."

"First thing is you have to see Dr. Greene a few more times. Just to ease my concern."

Lizzy let out a long breath. "Fine."

"Thank you," Cade said. "The second thing is I want your word you won't make any rash decisions about leaving."

"I'm not going to just take off," she said, lifting the shade as the sound of tires kicking up gravel caught her attention. "I might roam from station house to station house, but I'm not irresponsible and I have bills to pay. I need to know I've got the next job lined up. You don't have to worry about that."

"Good to know. Call me if you need anything at all."

"Thanks, Cade. I've got to run." She tapped the red end button on her cell. Echo occasionally stopped by unannounced on her way home from her parent's house, but she usually texted first. Quickly, she glanced at her phone.

No such text.

She pulled open the door, slightly disappointed there was no baby in Echo's arms. "What are you doing here?"

Echo raced across the yard and yanked Lizzy into her arms, hugging her as if the world had just ended.

"What's wrong? Are your parents okay?" Lizzy took her by the forearms and stepped back.

"They're fine," Echo said.

"Then who? Spencer? Andrea? What's got you so rattled?"

"Are you kidding me?"

Lizzy stared at her friend, who had this odd look of concern. "Why are you so upset?"

"Why are you not more upset? Jesus. Your parents could be set free in like a month."

Lizzy opened her mouth, but all that came out was the sound a dying cow would make during slaughter. She snapped it shut and tried again. This time, nothing. Perhaps the third time would be a charm. "How long have you known?"

"Seriously? Do you take me for an idiot?"

"No." Lizzy stepped aside, letting Echo into the kitchen. "I'm just a little surprised you never said anything to me."

"I almost did a few times. But I had to think about why you called yourself Lizzy." Echo arched a brow. "You hated that name when we were kids. If you were using it as an adult, it meant something, so I kept my mouth shut. I have a lot of respect for you I had to assume you had your reasons, though I hope it's not because you think I wouldn't like you or something because that would stupid." Echo took another glass and poured a bit of tequila for herself. "Do you mind? Spencer is at my folks and he said if I have too much, he'll come get me and drive me home."

"Help yourself." Lizzy took her glass and held it up. "I hadn't started yet, and I don't plan on getting shit-faced, but cheers." What a bizarre turn of events, but Morgan called it, as did Cade, and they were right. "I'm sorry I didn't tell you. Ever since I left this town thirteen years ago, I've been keeping that part of my life hidden from the world."

Echo shrugged. "I was pissed for about five

minutes. Hurt for maybe ten. But I understand why you would keep that part of your past hidden. Even from those who already knew about it." She sat at the table. "What are you going to do?"

"I don't know. I just got off the phone with Cade; he suggested I take some time off and get my head straight."

"Not a bad idea."

"Does everyone know I'm Eliza?"

"Spencer and his dad, as well as mine, but outside of that, I honestly don't know. It's not something any of us talk about. When you first came back, and we put it together, most of us had a conversation about it. But we all decided that because you went by Lizzy —a name you loathed—we figured if and when you were ready to talk about it, or trust us again with your identity, you'd open up."

"I don't deserve you." Lizzy eased into the chair across from her friend. "I always said if and when my folks went before a parole hearing, I'd go and testify as to why they shouldn't be set free any earlier than their sentence."

"Maybe that's what you should do."

Lizzy took a slow sip of tequila. It burned as it hit her throat. Something she wasn't used to happening. Normally, it went down like butter. She wasn't sure if it was because Echo hadn't ripped her a new asshole and acted as if she hadn't been betrayed.

Or if it was because Lizzy was actually contemplating going to that fucking hearing for real.

"I haven't had any contact with my parents since I testified in court as to what happened the night they set the fires. They wrote me letters. I didn't read a single one."

"Do you still have them?"

Lizzy nodded. "They are unopened in a shoebox in my closet. They stopped trying to contact me about the time I moved to Syracuse, though for all I know, things just aren't getting forwarded to me anymore. And frankly, I just don't care."

Echo tilted her head and downed half her glass. "I call bullshit."

"Excuse me?"

"Come on. Now that the charade is up and we can call on memory lane, I've known you since we were in grade school. You might have been older, but we were still friendly. As a matter of fact, I recall a couple of birthday sleepovers with a few mutual friends we both attended."

"What does that have to do with my parents and me not wanting to communicate with them?" Lizzy stared into the clear liquid. Flashes of her childhood filled her mind. One in particular kept playing over and over again, and she couldn't shut it off, no matter how hard she tried.

And she wanted it to stop.

Remembering the good times with her parents made it difficult to hate them.

Feeling the love and warmth they provided her as a child made her want to vomit.

She glanced outside. The same image of her father holding her upright on her bike and running down the street, encouraging her as she learned to ride a two-wheeler, continued to haunt her.

How could her folks just flip a switch and turn into horrible criminals? What made them do it? Losing their jobs wasn't the worst thing in the world. It wasn't like they were dirt poor. None of it made sense to her, and honestly, she didn't want to try to figure it out.

"Your parents were stand-up people. Everyone in this community was shocked, especially those who knew your parents. I remember how upset my dad had been when he found out and not just because he'd had Karen as student but because your parents had been at our house for dinner on more than one occasion. They were friends and he didn't see this coming. No one did. When your mom and dad were fired, they didn't act as if they were bitter."

"Oh, they were bitter, all right. They were so pissed off they forbade me from ever speaking to Karen again." Lizzy picked at her fingernail. It had been a long time since she'd told this part of the story and she wasn't sure she wanted to tell it now.

"I didn't know that."

"I didn't tell anyone. My parents were fired a week before the fire. They wouldn't let me out of the house. They'd gone crazy, but I was the only one who saw it. Experienced. It was surreal. I felt like I was living in the twilight zone."

"What do you mean by crazy?"

"They'd pulled down all the shades and locked the doors. If I wasn't freaked out enough, they took my cell and my computer. They wouldn't let me watch television, except for streaming. I didn't even know they got fired until after it happened. It seemed like all they did was sit at the kitchen table and yell at each other about what to do. Whenever I tried to talk to them about what happened, they told me to shut up and go to my room. I'd never seen them like that. It was as if they weren't even my parents. All I wanted to do was talk to my best friend."

Echo gasped, covering her mouth. "You were at Karen's place."

"I snuck out of my house after my parents said they were going to the store. I stuffed my bed with pillows, making it look like I was sleeping, which is ridiculously funny now because I'm not sure my parents' plan was to come back and get me."

"You don't know that."

"I don't care. And if they did, and I hadn't snuck out, and I knew what happened, I wouldn't have wanted to stay with them. They are cold-blooded killers."

Echo shook her head. "They swore up and down during that trial that they didn't know the Lands were home. They had stated they had spoken to them and were under the impression they had gone out to dinner and wouldn't be home for hours."

"And you think that makes what they did okay?" Lizzy's heart raced. Her blood boiled. "Are you trying to tell me you believe they should be out on the streets? Because that's ridiculous."

"Of course not. They absolutely deserved to go to prison for what they did. However, my dad said they were remorseful for their actions."

"Only because people died," Lizzy said, dabbing

the tears burning a river down her cheeks. "They planned the arson rampage. It was premeditated."

"But not the murders."

"That doesn't matter to me. They had to know it was possible for people to be in any of those buildings. And the point is: my parents aren't who I thought they were. They aren't the kind, loving people who I thought raised me. You don't just flip a switch and become arsonists." Lizzy flattened her hands on the table and leaned forward. "During that week, they were discussing things I didn't understand at the time, but I believe they lost their jobs because they were already doing something criminal, but by burning down the house, so to speak, they were able to cover all that up."

"Are you sure?"

"I can't be totally positive, but I remember hearing them say things like *they don't have proof*, or *we have to deal with it before they find the change in the books*, among other things. I just don't believe my parents were who they portrayed themselves to be."

"That very well could be the truth, but don't you want to find out? Maybe the letters they wrote have some answers to why they set the fires."

"According to the trial, they did so because they were falsely fired due to differences in management styles. They believed the Lands were going to tarnish their good names. We will never know the truth to because my parents killed the Lands, their daughter, and nearly killed me in the process." Lizzy held up her hand when Echo tried to say something. "And let's not forget, my parents went to jail with not a penny to their name and the Lands' business was missing money. Money that I might add is still missing that no one knows where it went, and I'm sorry, but I don't buy this bullshit that the Lands were stealing from themselves and my parents found out and were going to blame them for it, which is why they fired them."

"You think it's the other way around," Echo said as a statement of fact and not a question. "If that's the case, where did your parents put the money?"

"I have no idea."

"Don't you think that's something to figure out before they are released?" Echo reached across the table and grabbed Lizzy's hands. "This is a puzzle that has haunted this town for years. It's not just a question of why your parents set the fire, but what the hell happened to that money? Now that your parents are coming up for parole, it's going to be on everyone's minds."

"It's not my problem." Lizzy chugged the rest of

her tequila. "I should have changed my last name too."

"Look. I care about you. I've hated not being able to talk to you about all this, but out of respect, I've let it go. I can't do that anymore. Whether you want to believe it or not, this has been slowly killing you, and until you come to terms with what happened, which means at least trying to find some answers, you're going to spend the rest of your life with that bottle as your best friend." She pointed toward the half-empty tequila bottle on the counter.

Before Lizzy could counter a defense, her phone buzzed.

Morgan's name flashed on the screen.

"Why is my brother calling you?" Echo asked with a half-smile.

"No idea." She reached out to hit decline, but Echo snatched it.

"Morgan?" Echo answered.

"Echo? What are you doing answering Lizzy's phone?"

"I could ask you—"

"Oh, both of you shut the fuck up," Lizzy said. "Morgan, I'll call you after your sister leaves."

"Okay," Morgan said, and thankfully, the phone went dead.

"So, you told him who you are before me?" Echo asked with a slight tinge of sadness in her voice.

"No. He just confronted me on it before you did."

"Sorry. I shouldn't have said that." Echo stood and strolled across the small kitchen. She ran her fingers across the counter and stared out the window in the family room. "You know how hard it was for me to return here and admit my relationship was failing." Echo laughed. "Shit. I had screwed up my life so badly all because I thought I needed to go see the world." She turned and faced Lizzy. "Which I did. I honestly believe Spencer and I needed some space, but coming back here with my tail between my legs and having my fiancé basically leave me at the altar was absolutely humiliating."

"Not to be rude, but that's not the same thing." Lizzy understood her friend was simply trying to relate. However, it was apples to oranges, and frankly, Lizzy was done. At this point, all she wanted to do was lie on the sofa, eat popcorn, and watch mindless television.

"Oh. Trust me. I know. But I have a point." Echo leaned against the door. "I didn't know what Spencer was thinking or feeling because I didn't really let him in. Same thing with my family. I'd pushed them all away because I didn't want them to know that I was scared, but I came home anyway. I wanted them to know; I just didn't know how to tell them."

"Echo, you're talking babble to me." Lizzy loved Echo like a sister, but she tended to be long-winded.

With everything.

"First, you wanted all of us to know who you were, even though you didn't tell us."

Lizzy laughed. "Okay."

"Second." Echo held up two fingers. "You've kept the letters because deep down you want to read them, but maybe, just maybe, you need to do that in a safe place. Just like I needed to come home and be jilted at the altar with my family." Echo smiled. "Of course, Spencer was a nice surprise. But I think you get my point."

As ridiculous and rudimentary as Echo sounded, she made way too much sense, and that pissed Lizzy right the fuck off. She opened her mouth but quickly snapped it shut.

She had nothing.

"I'm here if you want someone to sit with you when you decide to look over those letters." She pointed out the window. "Spencer and Andrea are headed this way. Are you going to be okay?"

Lizzy nodded. She waved her phone. "I'm going to call your brother back, and then I'm going to watch a little TV, order a pizza, and get a good night's sleep. I've got to be at work early. Then I'm going to take a few days off. I was thinking I might go camping or something."

"You've got to be fucking kidding me? You? Sleep in a tent? This I have to see."

"Do you want to come?"

"Hell, yes, but I have to coordinate with Spencer, and I couldn't be gone for more than one night," Echo said with a smile so big she looked like a little girl entering Cinderella's palace.

"Let's plan it."

"I'll be in touch."

Lizzy stood and gave her friend a hug. "Thanks for forgiving me my lie."

"I love you, Lizzy. Call me if you need me."

"Thanks." Lizzy leaned against the doorjamb and waved to Spencer, who tucked a half-awake baby into her car seat. Lizzy wasn't ready to read those letters, but she was ready to start accepting the fact that people knew she was Eliza Cohen, and she was willing to embrace it.

6

---

*L*izzy dug her heels into the ground, gripping the empty hose. She glanced over her shoulder and nodded.

Troy Farren turned the lever and the white hose filled with water, snaking toward Lizzy. She pointed it toward the smoke oozing out of the broken window in a two-story house on Assembly Point. So far, the blaze was contained to one home, but this one was burning hot and fast and they needed to keep it under control.

She continued to work her section while Spencer worked his, and the rest of the team did their jobs, ensuring the safety of those around them. She inched closer, changing the angle of the water, tilting it higher.

Fletcher signaled to change positions. Troy helped her lift the running hose and move to a different section. The good news was that they knew no one was in that house.

Unfortunately, they also knew exactly what started the fire. Nothing worse than having to bring the fire marshal down on a twelve-year-old boy for playing with matches.

Troy tapped her shoulder. "We're shutting the water down for now."

"Okay," she yelled back. A minute later, the heavy hose felt like a feather. She recoiled it back to the engine and took a moment to take her helmet off and wipe the sweat off her brow. One of the things she liked about being a firefighter was that the majority of the calls weren't fires at all. The old saying was true about rescuing cats from trees.

And she'd rescued at least six in her career.

"Hey, Lizzy," Fletcher called. "You up for a walk-through?"

"Sure thing." She snagged her oxygen tank.

"Let me help." Troy took the apparatus and helped her attach it to her back. She pulled the face mask down and adjusted her hat. Giving Troy the thumbs-up, she made her way toward Fletcher.

"Let's go," Fletcher said.

She nodded. Walking a hot fire was always dangerous, but necessary. They needed to know a few things about the structure of the house and if the fire was really nothing but hot ash. "Anyone talk to the kid?" she asked.

"I did. Poor boy is scared shitless he's going to go to juvie and then prison for the rest of his life."

"At least he's frightened," she said.

Fletcher motioned toward the kitchen as they entered the house.

Thick smoke rose from the embers. Her feet crunched over the distressed wood, now so damaged it was nothing more than kindling. She glanced above her, making sure nothing would come down on her head, though it had been confirmed the fire began in the back room, which had been what the boy called the *gaming room*. When his mother came home, he tossed the hot matches and whatever he was burning into the trash and went to the kitchen to help with supper.

The next thing they knew, their house was on fire, and it quickly spread.

The family room had more smoke damage and now water damage than anything else, but still, this house would probably be unlivable for quite some time.

She met Fletcher in the hallway, and they made their way to the gaming room. Standing in the center of the door, she glanced at her co-worker. The damage was extensive, and the embers still burned hot. He cocked his head. They would need to pull one hose to the back and douse at least one more time.

Following Fletcher to the front of the house, a flash from her childhood filled her mind. She paused midstep as her heart stopped. Her chest tightened, and she found it difficult to breathe. Glancing over her shoulder, she blinked. She knew what she saw wasn't real, but try as she might, she couldn't stop the scene from playing out.

A man, carrying a young girl, came barreling down the stairs. He yelled something she couldn't understand, but she thought it might have something to do with the fact she was breathing. That, unlike the others, she was still alive.

Alive.

That word echoed in Lizzy's mind.

"Lizzy, let's go."

She shook her head. "Coming." She stepped through the front door and pulled off her helmet and then her mask.

"What happened in there?" Fletcher asked.

"Nothing. I just wanted to make sure the stairs were secure."

Fletcher arched a brow, but then nodded. "Troy, get the hose and take it around back. One more shot, and we should be good."

"On it," Troy said.

"Go help with the equipment," Fletcher said. "I need to go talk with the fire marshal."

Lizzy put her oxygen tank away and tossed her coat on the back seat of the ladder truck. She snagged a water bottle and chugged. What made this fire more difficult than others was that it had been started by a kid, and it did have the potential of spreading to other houses, causing massive destruction and loss of life.

Oh hell, all fires did that, but she was also sensitive to those involving kids, no matter the circumstances.

Out of the corner of her eye, she noted Bradley Bryant, Spencer's dad, and the fire marshal heading in her direction.

Fuck.

She really didn't feel like talking to him or reliving any tender moment he might have for saving her life.

"Lizzy Cohen?" he asked as he closed the gap. "Eliza Cohen?"

"Yes, sir," she said, stretching out her arm. "It's been a long time."

"Actually, it's been three weeks, but we don't need to get into that." He shook her hand. "I thought you looked familiar when Cade hired you, and then it hit me about a year ago. I wish you would have said something."

"I'm sorry, sir." She really didn't want to get into this here, but he wasn't leaving her any choice, and he was the fucking fire marshal. What was she going to do, tell him to take a goddamned hike? "I was trying to put that part of my life behind me."

"I can understand that, though hard to do considering what's about to happen."

She nodded.

"I know this is a shitty time to do this, but I'd like to talk to you about your parents' hearing. Maybe early next week?"

"I can do that," she said.

"Good. I'll call you later to set it up." Bradley planted his hands on his hips and glanced over his shoulder. "I have one more big ask."

"What's that?"

"Will you talk to the young man who started the fire?"

She gasped. "Me. Why?" She wasn't cut out to talk to kids, much less emotional kids who just burned down their house. "And what the hell do you want me to say to him?"

"Assure him that when accidents happen, we don't send people to jail and that my investigation is a formality since he admitted to everything. Just reassure him that he's going to be okay."

"You still haven't told me why you want me to do it because any one of us could come across the same way."

Bradley shook his head. "First, you're the only female, and I understand from his mother, he has daddy issues."

She had no idea why that mattered, but who was she to argue.

"Second, I personally think it will be good for you."

She opened her mouth, but he raised his hand.

"I'm not giving you a pass and don't make me go and call your captain."

"Yes, sir." She took a towel and wiped her face. She had no choice but to go talk to the young man.

She stepped from the ladder truck and looked around the yard.

The young boy sat on the tailgate of a neighbor's truck, wrapped in a blanket with his mother. She adjusted her suspenders and pulled her ponytail tighter. She nodded to Jake Prichard, the state trooper who'd been the first to arrive. She'd met Jake a few times over the years with Tristan as well as Jared, who was their boss.

"Hey, Lizzy," Jake said.

"The fire marshal wants me to talk to the boy."

Jake nodded. "He's pretty shaken up and scared to death of men," Jake said. "I found out from his mom that his dad was a cop over in Utica and used to beat the crap out of both of them. His old man was arrested about six months ago, but the boy has been acting out ever since. All reports show he's a good kid, but this is the kind of event that could really destroy him."

"You ain't kidding," she said. She slipped her arms through her suspender straps. "Anything else I should know?"

"His mother said he's been fascinated with fire for a long time. He watches a lot of search and rescue shows and has made comments about wanting to be a firefighter when he grows up."

"Sounds like he's trying to understand the element," she said, relating to the kid's thirst for knowledge. After the fires her parents set, she studied fires for the next couple of years. Mostly arsons, but she wanted to get into the game, and during her youth, she set a few fires herself, though none got out of control and she was smart enough not to drop a hot match in a garbage can. "Thanks for the intel. Wish me luck."

She sucked in a deep breath and closed the gap. She smiled at the young boy and his mother. "Hi. I'm Lizzy," she said. "Is it okay if I speak to your son for a few moments?"

"About what?"

"I'd like to talk to him about maybe visiting the station and offer a lending ear if he needs someone to talk to about his passion."

"He's a good boy. He just doesn't know how to deal with what happened with his dad. He actually wants to be a fireman."

"I might be able to help him. I had a bit of a troubled adolescence and came into this profession through the back door, so to speak. I'd like to help him if I can and with your permission."

The young mother nodded and stepped aside.

"Thank you." Lizzy inched closer.

The boy wrapped the blanket tighter. "Am I in trouble?"

"I don't think so," she said, sitting down next to him. "You know, when I was a kid, I was fascinated by fires. I had a police band radio, and whenever there was a fire, I would try to make sure I was there. Everyone thought I was crazy, but I wanted to see the firefighters at work."

"I didn't set the fire on purpose."

"I believe you," she said. "Can I tell you a secret?"

"Sure."

"I became a firefighter because my parents purposely started a fire that hurt people."

The boy snapped his gaze up and stared at her with wide eyes.

"But even after they were caught, I still found myself playing with fire, even though I knew how dangerous it could be. I wanted to understand how the flames worked. I was just so fascinated by it all."

The young man sat up a little taller. "I am too. I only wanted to watch as it made its way down the match, but my mom came home. I had to put it out, as well as my candles. I'm not allowed to burn anything while she's gone."

"That's a good rule," Lizzy said. "If you'd like, I

can arrange for you to visit the station house and have a tour."

"You would do that for me? After what I've done?"

"Yeah. I would." She nodded. "That doesn't mean your mom isn't going to ground you. Or that there won't be consequences, because you do need to take responsibility for what you did, but everyone knows you didn't mean to do it. And I think we all know this will never happen again."

"No. Never."

"Good." She ruffled the hair on his head. "I'll get my contact information for your mom. You can call me anytime, okay?"

"Thanks."

"Anytime." She stood and meandered back toward the ladder truck. That went better than she could have ever expected. It actually felt good. It gave her even more purpose in her career and a connection to another person in a way that was totally unexpected.

Oddly, it made her want to reach out to Morgan, whom she missed, and that bothered her in a way she couldn't understand. He was meant to be a fling. More or less a one-night stand that wandered in and out of her bed whenever he was in town, and the mood struck her.

Or him.

Or both.

It wasn't supposed to be a yearning thing. She wasn't supposed to think about him when she closed her eyes at night or have him be the first thought when she woke up in the morning.

But all she wanted to do was call him and fall asleep listening to his voice.

Morgan kicked off his shoes and tossed his keys by the front door. In the five years he'd lived in this house, he'd never felt lonely.

Until right now.

He hated that his mother had been right.

He missed Lizzy more than he even dared to admit to himself.

She made him want to rethink his life choices, and that was just preposterous. He liked his carefully crafted world. He spent most of his time alone, which he loved. He could go down and see his family anytime he wanted.

Which he loved just as much.

And he could keep civilization at arm's length, and that kept him fucking sane.

He wasn't a people person.

Sure, he was a family man. As in he loved his brothers, his sister, her husband and their kid, and his parents. Along with his extended family, which included the family he chose.

Outside of that, he didn't give a shit.

He snagged a frozen dinner from the freezer and popped it into the microwave. He pulled a beer and cracked it open, taking a good gulp. The bubbles tickled the back of his throat. It was exactly what he needed after a long shift.

Twelve hours to be exact.

And now that it was approaching ten at night, all he wanted was a couple of beers, some food, and some sleep.

He tapped his foot while he waited. He was a shitty cook, so he didn't even bother. Nine out of ten times, these meals weren't that great, but he'd run out of the ones his mother had prepared for him, so they would have to do.

God, he was pathetic.

He pulled back the wrapping and dumped the meat and potatoes onto a plate. He got himself a second beer because he knew he'd need it and made himself comfortable on his sofa in the family room.

His home was about two thousand square feet. It overlooked the rich hillside leading up to the Dix Range and in the fall, the colorful change in leaves was a sight to behold. His nearest neighbor was about two miles away and that was just fine by him.

He scarfed down his dinner in seconds. It wasn't about flavor, because if he focused on that, he'd have to admit the damn shit tasted like cardboard. It was all about filling his belly. He finished his first beer and placed the empty in the recycle bin before washing his dish and leaving it to dry in the rack.

Time to watch a little TV before heading to bed.

This was his routine. He told himself this was how he liked his life. That he had no desire to change it.

He pointed the remote at the television, but before he could hit the on button, his cell phone rang.

Lizzy.

His heart skipped a beat, and his breath caught in his throat. He would consider changing everything for her and that thought scared the shit out of him.

"Hey. Is everything okay?" he asked. Since her parents' hearing had been set and everyone had admitted to knowing who she was, things had changed for her.

And not always for the good.

At least in her eyes.

He wished he could be there to help her navigate all this.

"I just had a weird night."

"How so?"

"Had a house fire caused by a kid, but that wasn't the weird part. Bradley Bryant made me talk to the boy who started it."

"Why?"

"Doesn't really matter. The point is it got me thinking again about my parents. The hearing and all the times they tried to reach out to me."

"Are you thinking about talking to your folks before the hearing?" He raised his beer to his lips and took a long swig.

"I am."

"That might not be the worst thing in the world."

"I don't want to face them." There was a slight tremble in her voice. He couldn't blame her, and he'd be scared too. "It's been thirteen years."

"I can come with you and hold your hand."

She let out a nervous laugh. "I don't think that's necessary."

"I don't mind. Besides, I don't think you should go alone."

"I was thinking about calling them. Seeing them face-to-face is not something I believe I can handle, even with moral support."

"I've got your back no matter what you need." He'd do whatever she wanted, which was a concept that was completely, utterly, and totally foreign to him. Sure, he would do whatever was necessary to aid another ranger. Or a family member. However, she was neither. "But a face-to-face meeting might be the better bet."

"Why do you say that?"

"A plethora of reasons. One being to see their facial reactions to whatever it is you want to say or ask. That can be very telling and if you have an outsider, they can help interpret since you might be too close to the situation."

"Are you volunteering?"

"I am."

"I need to think on that," she said. "What are you doing?"

"Watching television, drinking a beer, and talking to you, why?" His FaceTime went off.

Lizzy.

He tapped his cell. "Well, hello there, beautiful."

"I look like shit." She brushed her long hair from her face, tucking it behind her ears. She didn't have a stitch of makeup on, but she didn't need. She laid on her bed and the moonlight filtered in through the window, showing off her big blue eyes. "Is that a deer head behind you?" She squinted.

He glanced over his shoulder. "Yes. It is. But I didn't kill it if that makes you feel any better."

"It does, I guess."

He chuckled. "And for the record, you look absolutely gorgeous." He winked.

"You need glasses."

"I see just fine." He sipped his beer. "You are a sight for sore eyes."

"So are you."

"Admitting this is a little strange, but I've missed you." He stared at her angelic face, wishing he could pull her close.

"Yeah, I miss you too."

"Where does that leave us?" he asked.

"Up shit creek without a paddle," she said. "I'm sorry. This is going to come out ass-backward, but I don't like feeling this way."

"I can totally understand that," he said. "But at least we can agree we're both uncomfortable about caring for one another."

"What the fuck are you talking about? I meant about the kid and how talking to him made me feel."

"Right, because that's what we were just talking about." He laughed. "If it makes you sleep better at night to tell yourself that, okay, I'll let you."

"It does." She sighed. "Can I ask a really huge favor?"

"Of course."

"Will you stay with me until I fall asleep tonight?"

His heartbeat picked up. She had to be the strongest woman he knew, yet she needed him to watch over her for one night. "I can do that."

"I need to know you will stay with me for as long as possible. That you won't hang up on me just because I drifted off."

He stood, taking his beer and his phone up the stairs and into his bedroom. "I'm yours for the night. Make sure your phone is charging and we can even wake up together if you'd like."

"I don't want some weird sexting thing. I just want to fall asleep with you."

"I understand."

"Do you?"

"Yes. Just you and me and the stars." He flipped the screen, showing off his skylight. "Isn't that beautiful?"

"Oh, my God. It's fucking gorgeous," she whispered.

"I'll make sure you get that view again in a second." He flipped the screen back, setting his phone on the nightstand. He lifted his shirt over his head and undid the button of his jeans.

"I kind of like this view," she whispered.

He groaned. "No peep show. No sexting. No weird kinky shit." He shed his pants, pulled back the covers, and climbed into bed. Pulling in his cell, he propped it up on a pillow, giving her partial access to the skylight, and him, because he was just arrogant enough to believe she went with the video because she wanted to see his face. "Now, close your eyes and drift off to sleep, knowing I'm right here, watching over you."

"Thank you, Morgan. I owe you."

"You owe me absolutely nothing." He pulled his covers to his chin and turned off all his lights except the one next to his bed. "Good night, Lizzy."

"You'll stay here until I'm asleep?"

"I'm going to fall asleep with you."

"Thank you."

"It's my pleasure," he said. And he meant it. It was almost as good as having her right next to him, and one day, he hoped that would come true. "Close your eyes."

She did as instructed.

"Sleep, Lizzy."

"Good night, Morgan."

He sipped his beer while watching her fade off into dreamland. As soon as he was sure she was sound asleep, he set his empty longneck on the nightstand and closed his eyes, leaving the light on as well as his cell, just in case she awoke and needed him. "Sweet dreams, my love," he whispered. "Soon we'll be together. I promise."

7

"*L*izzy, could you come to the conference room?" Cade called from the lower level of the station house.

"I'll be right there." Lizzy took her plate and neatly tucked it in the dishwasher. She snagged a mug and filled it with coffee. This meeting would require caffeine. Actually, a shot of tequila would be a better choice, but this would have to do under the circumstances. Carefully, she took the steps as fast as she could as not to spill the hot, bitter liquid. "Hey, Captain," she said. "Marshal Bryant." She shook the fire marshal's hand.

"Thanks, Cade, for letting me borrow Lizzy for a few moments."

"No problem," Cade said. "She's one of the best on my crew."

"You say that about everyone you've groomed here."

"That's true." Cade smiled proudly. "And you and my mother are the ones who trained me." He turned on his heel and strolled off toward his office.

Bradley, the fire marshal, waved his hand into the conference room. He carried a file in his other, along with his phone. "You're working under one of the best men I know in the department."

"He's certainly the best captain I've had so far in my career."

"The fact you want to leave saddens me." Bradley took a seat at the head of the table. He crossed his legs and rested his hands on the arms of the chair.

"I move around a lot. I've always wanted to see different places. Experience different things."

"Cade tends to take it personally when someone wants to leave his house."

"I know," she said. "But if I were to go, it would be about me and no one else."

Bradley nodded, setting his cell and the file on the table. "I thought it would be best to meet here and talk about your parents since I know this is a safe place for you."

That had to be the weirdest statement anyone had ever made to her, but she'd go with it. "I appreciate the concern for my comfort. I haven't spoken to or about my folks since the trial. Obviously, coming back here and the fact they will be at a parole hearing in a little over a week and a half, has forced many conversations about them."

Bradley's phone buzzed. He glanced at it quickly. "Is it okay with you if two state troopers join us?"

Her throat suddenly became dry, and she couldn't swallow. "Um. Sure. But why?"

"I'll explain in a bit." He tapped on the screen. "Do you know Jake Prichard and Tristan Reid?

"Yes. I rent Tristan's modular home he's friends with Morgan. I've also worked with both of them on a call or two."

"Good. They are… well, here they are." Bradley stood, waving Tristan and Jake, who wore their uniforms, into the conference room.

Lizzy felt as though she'd been cornered, and she wanted to run. She stiffened her spine and sucked in a deep breath, letting it out slowly through her nose.

"Good to see you again," Jake said.

Tristan squeezed her shoulder.

"Let me get right to the point since we're all on the clock, and that siren could ring at any time."

Bradley reached across the table and put his hand over hers and squeezed. "I always wished I could have done more for you."

"Are you kidding? You saved my life." Lizzy swallowed a sob. "I do know you're the one who carried me out that day."

Bradley lowered his head. "You and Karen were in the back upstairs bedroom. It was filled with thick black smoke. The flames had burst through the floorboards. I was surprised anyone could have survived the smoke. When I got to you girls, there was only supposed to be one of you. I found Karen first. She was already gone. I went to lift her, and I heard this faint cough. You had wedged yourself under the bed and were trying to breathe through a blanket. You were barely conscious. I checked Karen for a pulse again." Bradley swiped at his cheeks. "The ones we lose, they stay with us forever and I had to make a decision. You still had a pulse. She didn't. The structure was about to crumble like a house of cards."

Lizzy knew that struggle all too well. There was nothing anyone could say or do right now that would change things or even make Bradley feel any better. All she could do was hold his hand and wait.

A minute passed, and Bradley lifted his head.

"Here's the thing. There was a lot of accusations tossed around during the trial."

"Excuse me, Bradley," Jake said. "Maybe you should backtrack one more step and add that there was one big rumor before the fire."

"Yes. Yes. Good point." Bradley nodded.

"I wasn't oblivious to some shit talk." Lizzy twisted her ponytail. "My parents went off on some conspiracy theory that they were falsely fired, and all they were trying to do was make sure the Lands didn't try to tarnish their good name, which makes no sense at all."

"It makes more sense than you think." Bradley opened the file and thumbed through some paperwork. "Before I go any further, I must ask you a tough question."

"It's an easy question. My parents belong in prison. They shouldn't be let out."

Bradley let out a long breath. "The arson case has been closed for years, but there are some unanswered questions about some other things, and I've been secretly digging with the help of some friends."

Tristan and Jake waved.

"And a few others," Tristan added. "You've met our boss, Jared. He was there that night too."

"I didn't know that," she said, wondering where the hell all of this was going.

"Many of the Lands employees stated that Ross and Monica Land had been acting weird the week before they fired your parents. There was talk about problems with money. After the fire, while dealing with the estate, it was found that a lot of money was missing from those two dealerships."

"My parents were the finance people," she said, taking a few of the pages that Bradley handed her. "This isn't new information."

"Nope. It's not. But it's still an open case. A cold one and the district attorney isn't doing anything with it because there is really no evidence." Tristan leaned back in his chair. "It all went up in smoke, so to speak."

"Everything at this point is hearsay," Jake added. "During the trial, your parents tried to paint the picture that the Lands would make it look like your folks were stealing from the dealerships. If they had not been caught going back to the scene because of you, they were trying to set up the Lands for the arson."

"I knew that," Lizzy said. "And I knew about the money rumors. I get the feeling that you know more."

"We have one thing that was not allowed in as evidence in any hearing regarding the fire or trying to pin your parents for embezzlement," Bradley said.

"I'm not following," Lizzy said.

Jake tapped the table with his knuckle. "There was a good couple of million missing from those dealerships, and no one can find a paper trail."

"Because it was destroyed in the fire," Lizzy said. "So what am I looking at?"

"Phone records. Specifically between you and Karen," Bradley said.

Lizzy snapped her gaze toward the fire marshal. "What the hell does that have to do with anything?"

"Two things," Bradley said. "Your parents testified that they had no idea you were at Karen's house and that they were driving home from a dinner when they saw the fire."

Lizzy nodded. "Though I told everyone that was a lie because, to my knowledge, they had no dinner plans, and I had just snuck out of the house after telling Karen not to come to me."

"In a statement you made to police, your parents confiscated your phone," Jake said.

"They had," she muttered.

"Your phone was put into an evidence box, where it's been sealed." Tristan leaned forward, pressing his hands on the table. "Here's where it gets interesting. "One of the reasons your phone was tossed out for being irrelevant was because it really had nothing to do with the arson, but the defense was able to prove that the prosecutor obtained some information by using improper sources."

"Just get to the point," she said.

"Your parents had your cell with them the entire night, so they were able to ping their whereabouts. Before they started the fires, they went to Albany."

"Why the hell would they do that, and why didn't they have their own cells?" she asked.

"Either they were brilliant and wanted everyone to believe they were at home, or they just forgot them," Bradley said. "But there were also some phone calls made from your cell that don't make sense."

She rubbed her temples. "If you've been secretly looking for answers to this fucking weird puzzle, why have you waited until now to bring it to my attention if you've known who I was all along?" This answer should be interesting.

"Out of respect," Bradley said. "And you were just an innocent little girl. But now that your parents are about to go before the parole board, and the fact they've been exemplary inmates, finding God and all that—"

"Wait. What?" She grabbed the entire file and started thumbing through it. "No fucking way did my parents find Jesus." Her folks might have been kind and loving, and she had a great childhood up until she didn't, but they hated organized religion.

Both of them.

Resented the hell out of the church would have been an understatement, but they both refused to go.

"Your parents always seemed like good people until that fire," Bradley said. "That's what makes this so hard, but I can't ignore what's sitting in front of me, and I don't believe them when they say they didn't know the Lands were in that house when they burned it down." Bradley folded his arms across his chest. "I think they stole millions, and it's sitting somewhere waiting for them, and I sure as hell don't want to let them get their hands on it."

"I can't agree with you more," she said. "How do we access to that phone so I can open it up and check out those numbers?"

Jake pushed a piece of paper in front of her. "This is a list of the numbers. Most are disconnected. This one went to a brokerage firm, and Mr. Halfax answered, but we don't know the connection because he said he had no idea who your parents were, and we have no record of him having any business dealings with your folks or the Lands."

"He was my dad's investor guy. I remember him because he always smelled like he'd been out fishing all day." She pinched the bridge of her nose. "I didn't like that guy."

"This number went to a Louis Amber," Jake said.

She tapped her temple. "I think that was one of my dad's golf buddies. A rich dude that lived in Saratoga."

"That would be correct. He says he's never heard of your dad either, and his number wasn't in your dad's cell," Tristan said with an arched brow. "Did your parents take your cell away a lot?"

"That was their go-to grounding ritual, so yeah, a fair amount."

"Did you notice any weird things on it when you got it back?"

She shook her head. "I changed my passcode every time they took it, but I know they could see whatever was on it."

"They must have had some spyware or something on it because that phone was used more for them than for you, but we can't prove it, and it's dead evidence now."

"I might have something," she said, closing her eyes, hoping the tears didn't push through her lids. She blinked. "My parents wrote me a ton of letters. I've never opened a single one."

"Why not?" Tristan asked.

"The last time I saw them, they begged me to forgive them. Begged me to tell the judge and anyone who would listen that they would never do anything to anyone on purpose. They told me they'd be lost without me and that if I were a good little girl, everything would be all right. It was that last statement that made me shiver and turned my blood cold. It made feel like if I didn't do what they wanted, I was bad. And I realized they'd been like that my whole life. I didn't want to hear their lies and I don't want them in my life."

"Do they still write to you?" Bradley asked.

"Funny you should mention that. The only address they have for me is Buffalo. It takes a while for all my forwarding to get caught up to me. I happened to get a box full the other day."

"Maybe you should open them," Tristan said.

She nodded. "I think I might attend that hearing after all."

———

Morgan spent two days driving himself crazy. Lizzy kept telling him she was fine, that having people know who she was and her parents' pending hearing wasn't affecting her one bit, but he knew better. She had a tightness to her voice that hadn't been there before. He had no plans to come to Lake George for another week, but he couldn't take it anymore.

He had to see Lizzy.

And not just on FaceTime.

Gripping the steering wheel, he took the turn onto Mason Road a little too harshly.

He flipped off the headlights and rolled to a stop next to Lizzy's small SUV. Thank God she was home, though, he could get a good tongue-lashing for having the nerve to show up unannounced. He got the impression that was something she didn't appreciate, but she kept downplaying her emotions, and that didn't bode well with him.

As quietly as he could, he closed the car door and went to the front entrance of her modular home. He used his knuckles and tapped three times.

Nothing.

He repeated a few times.

Nothing.

Gently, he nudged the door, but it was locked.

He pulled out his cell and pulled up the text chain.

Morgan: *Was just thinking about you. What are you doing?*

Bubbles immediately appeared.

Lizzy: *Hanging out at home. I have to work tomorrow at six. I'm pulling a double and then I've a few days off. I was going to text you when I got ready for bed.*

Home? He glanced around the dark yard and saw nothing but fireflies and stars lighting up the night sky.

Morgan: *Watching TV?*

Lizzy: *You're being oddly nosy. But no. I'm dangling my feet in the lake.*

He let out a long breath of relief. He stuffed his cell in his back pocket and strolled down the path toward the dock in front of her house.

She sat with her back to him. The moon cast a white shadow that stretched from one side of the bay all the way across, rolling with the slight ripples the warm breeze caused, ending at her toes. She wore her long hair up in a messy bun with some strands cascading down her back in soft curls.

"Hey," he said softly.

She jerked, twisting her body. "Jesus, Morgan. What the fuck are you doing here? You scared the crap out of me."

"I wasn't trying to." He pushed a small shoebox out of the way and sat beside her. "How are you holding up?"

"I really wish everyone would stop asking me that, including you."

He took her chin with his thumb and forefinger, tilting her head, giving him access to those gorgeous plump lips. Thankfully, she didn't push him away and participated in the kiss. "It's a legit question and you're the one who calls me every night."

"Maybe, but it's still annoying." She let out a long breath. "I only call because it's at night when I'm reminded that the hearing is on my fucking birthday and I'm going to come face-to-face with my murdering parents."

"I know." He looped his arm around her and pulled her close. "It sucks, but there is nothing you can do about that."

"Cade, the shrink, Echo, they all think I'm doing the right thing. But the closer we get to the date, the more my head hurts."

"You keep telling me you don't want to talk about it, but you have to deal with all of it." He lifted the bottle of tequila next to her. "And this isn't helping."

"I have had one shot and I'm actually done." Lizzy shook her head. "I honestly thought I could go through life and never deal with this, but I'm realizing you were right."

He kissed her temple. "About what?"

"That I've been drinking to avoid my feelings and that I've been slowly working my way across this state until I landed here." She shifted, catching his gaze. "But there's more."

He wished he could take away all the heartache she'd endured during her life. "What do you mean?"

"I think part of me was sad no one recognized me."

"We all did."

"Okay. Then I was upset that no one said anything, and I know that's ridiculous and on me because it was a stupid game that only fed into the idea that I was irrelevant."

"Holy shit. Why the fuck would you think that?" He cupped her cheeks. "That is the farthest thing from the truth."

She leaned into his palm and gave him a half-smile. "I know that now. But it's weird having everyone look at me and see Eliza, the little girl who survived a fire that was set by her parents and killed three people, and I don't like it. They look at me with a combination of pity and confusion."

"I don't know who *these* people are that you're

talking about, but no one I know feels that way about you."

"Maybe not. But then there are these." She lifted the box. "The letters from my parents. And there are more that came the other day. Bradley, Tristan, and all his trooper buddies want me to open them. They think it might have information into where all the missing millions went."

"I see," Morgan said, jumping to his feet. He took the box in one hand and helped her up with his other. "Let's go read them."

"You don't have to do that."

"I don't have to watch you fall asleep either, but I do it."

She laughed. "It sounds so weird when you put it like that."

"You did once call me strange."

---

8

*L*izzy tossed another letter onto the coffee table. That had been ten she'd read so far, and Morgan was on his sixth. She had to have a good two hundred to comb through. If not more. She stretched her arms over her head and let out a long breath. "These aren't telling us anything other than my parents want me to believe they never meant me to get caught in the middle of this. They repeat it like a million times."

"You were their daughter, and as odd as it may sound, just because someone is a criminal it doesn't mean they aren't capable of loving people."

Leave it to Morgan to bring in the logical bullshit that only added to her confusion. Nothing made sense other than her parents were guilty as hell. The only thing they didn't know was that their daughter had been in that house, but their intent was to harm, and they had planned the fires.

That was premeditation right there, and at least should have gotten them a heavier sentence.

Morgan pulled out his cell and set it on the table. He tapped the screen.

"What are you doing?"

"Calling Tristan."

It rang three times before he picked up. "Hey, what's up?" Tristan asked.

"What exactly are we looking for in these letters to Lizzy from her parents?"

"Clues to where they hid the money," he said matter-of-factly. "Anything that might lead us to the proof they embezzled from the dealerships and keep them from being paroled."

Lizzy twisted her hair through her fingertips. "Why? Why do you or anyone else care so much about keeping my parents in jail? What did they ever do to you?"

Morgan glared at her as if she had eight heads.

She shrugged. It seemed like a legit question. The entire town was in an uproar over the looming hearing and she was the only one that had anything at stake. The Lands were gone, and they had no family in the area. No other children and neither Ross or Monica had any siblings. Besides, her parents hadn't tried to murder anyone else, so why did they care so much about the damned money?

"Are you at Lizzy's?" Tristan asked.

"We are," Morgan said.

"I'll be over in fifteen." The phone went dead.

"What the fuck was that all about?" She pushed herself to her feet and shook out her leg, which had fallen asleep. She hated that feeling of pins and needles.

Morgan handed her one of the letters. "I think my buddy has been keeping a few key points from you." He rubbed the back of his neck. "Mind if I help myself to a beer and a bag of chips?"

"Be my guest." She flicked the paper and started reading.

Dear Eliza,

It was so good to see you in court today. We hope you will be given this letter before you leave. We totally understand why you had to say the things you did. You're just a kid, and being honest is what you should be doing, and we're proud of you for that.

Jesus. What a fucked-up thing to say.

We know this is hard for you, losing your best friend that way. You have to understand we never meant for this to happen. It wasn't supposed to go down like that. We had a job to do. The Lands knew it and they chose to do things differently.

She dropped her hand to the side. "This makes no fucking sense."

"Let me see." Morgan lifted the letter. "Damn," he muttered.

"What the hell in God's name does it mean?"

"I think we're about to find out." Morgan opened the door and let Tristan in.

"Wow. This place looks great. Better than when I lived here," Tristan said.

"It's feeling crowded, and I can't breathe." Lizzy pushed past him and out the door, but not before she snagged the bottle of tequila, ignoring Morgan's evil eye. "Let's sit at the picnic table. There's more beer in the fridge or grab yourself a glass if you want some of this." She waved the bottle in the air.

"I'm good, but thanks." Tristan made himself comfortable in one of the chairs by the fire pit.

So did Morgan, so who was she to go against the grain?

"What are you really looking for and don't fucking lie," Morgan said with a bit of disdain dripping from his words. "She's been through enough."

"What did you find in the letters?"

"Answer my question first, and then we'll discuss what her parents sent," Morgan said.

Lizzy had never seen him behave so defensively, especially with his buddies. She couldn't decide if she liked it or resented it. This was her battle, not his, but she wasn't sure how to handle Tristan or what had gotten Morgan's panties in a wad to begin with, other than the one letter, which she couldn't figure out.

"A connection was made to the Lands and the Mortelli family about a year before the fires. They were under FBI investigation." Tristan folded his arms and stared at the sky.

"You've got to be shitting me," Morgan said. "How did that not come up in trial?"

"The Feds were interested in the Mortellis, not the Lands or Lizzy's parents," Tristan said. "They were small potatoes and maybe a means to an end. From all that we've read or been able to gather, the agent in charge of the case came in, looked at the information, talked to the people involved, and because everything was destroyed in those fires, they moved on."

Lizzy couldn't sit down for this conversation. She stood and paced in front of the pit. She took a small sip from the tequila bottle. It soured in her belly. "Basically, the Lands and my parents worked for a mob family? That's the theory?"

"In a nutshell, yes," Tristan said.

"One letter I read implied they had a job to do, and the Lands knew it and chose to do things a different way," she said. "Do you think the Lands knew the fires were going to happen?"

"They could have," Tristan said.

"But then why stay at home?" she asked.

"You know, we can ask these questions and keep guessing, or we can get the letters." Morgan jumped to his feet. "Feel like doing a little light reading? If that's okay with Lizzy."

"Hey. The more the merrier," Lizzy mumbled.

"Brooke is with my mom and I don't expect her home for another hour, so sure, why not," Tristan said.

Lizzy went back to the table where Morgan spread out the letters. She arranged them by date, and she chose to dig into the most recent ones, only because she didn't want to dive that far into her past.

She also hoped that she would be the one to find the smoking gun. She wanted to be the one to put an end to all this insanity. Also, if the answer had been in the earlier letters, then it was one more reason to kick herself.

Of course, she knew there would be sprinkles throughout.

She flattened one of the letters and ran her hand over the creases.

Dear Lizzy,

We heard you're going by that now. That's not even close to Eliza. Not to mention someone once tried to give you that as a nickname and you hated it. So did we. Are you that ashamed of who you are? Of where you came from?

We're assuming you are, or why choose a name that got under you skin?

You don't know anything, even if you think you do... you don't.

But if it makes you feel better, we'll call you Lizzy. We just want our little girl to be happy, healthy, and provided for.

Something you haven't let us do and we want to make sure that happens; you just have to find the Easter eggs.

"Morgan. Read this." She pushed the paper in front of him and rested her hand on his thigh as if touching him would give her the support she needed.

"Yeah. I've seen that a few times in other letters. It's as if they are trying to tell you to find the hidden eggs. Which could mean where they hid the stolen money."

"We should look to see if the dates of the letter match up to the postmarks," Tristan said. "If they don't, maybe it's bank routing number or maybe a safety deposit box."

"Look at the cop go," Lizzy said with a little too much sarcasm laced in her words. "Sorry. I'm tired, and the tequila isn't working for me like it used to."

"You remind me a lot of my wife when I first met her, only she used anger the same way you use, well, that bottle. But once she figured out what she was really upset over, she settled. Just don't ever look at her cross-eyed. She'll bite your head off."

"I'll remember that." Lizzy took another letter, cross referencing the dates. "Yeah. Some of these don't match up."

"And another thing. Did you notice they often made these little squiggly things by their signatures?" Morgan asked. "My parents put notes in my lunches when I was a kid. It was so embarrassing by the time I hit middle school to have a note with a little smiley face from my mom on it with the words *I love you my little Morgan*. Did your parents do that?"

Lizzy shook her head. "No. Not once." She picked up some of the letters. "Some of these are letters, and some are numbers."

"It's a bank," Tristan said. "Or maybe a broker's name. But I bet all this is telling us where the money that they stole is."

"Wait a second." Lizzy twisted her hair into a braid. "If the Lands worked for this crime family too, wouldn't they have been in on this money thing?"

Tristan waved his finger. "You know, the Lands could have been the ones taking the money, and your parents could have been trying to get it back."

"By killing them?" Lizzy asked. She swallowed a guttural sob.

Tristan nodded. "They worked for a mob family. One much like what you see portrayed in the movie *The Godfather*. And that's where your phone might also be a key because perhaps you and Karen weren't supposed to be killed at all." Tristan leaned forward. "In many of these families, children are untouchables. So, if you told Karen not to bother, you were on your way over—"

"That doesn't fly with the direction you're taking this," she interrupted Tristan. "Because that would mean my parents would have never burned down their house."

Morgan tapped her shoulder. "But in numerous letters they mentioned they had a job to do but the Lands chose to do it differently. Maybe they communicated with Ross and Monica and told them they better move the kids because this was going down. The Lands chose not to."

"That also suggests murder was not the end game," Lizzy said.

"Might not have been," Tristan agreed. "But here's something else we need to be worried about."

"What's that?" Morgan asked.

"We've seen some of the Mortelli people in the area. This is making Jared very nervous."

"It's making me more than a little skittish," she muttered. "I guess I should have really changed my name."

Morgan squeezed her hand.

"I don't think you have anything to worry about," Tristan said. "However, we don't know if your parents are on good terms with the Mortellis or not. My guess is that they are because they are still alive. Or at the very least, they have something the Mortellis want."

"It all comes down to the money and if they were skimming off the top?" Lizzy asked.

"Someone was. The real question is: were the Lands skimming and the Mortellis ordered your parents to set the fires, or were your parents and they were doing whatever they had to in order to cover their tracks?"

"Based on these letters I'd have to say it was the latter," she said.

"Only, Jared found a dozen fires in upstate New York that fit your parents MO and all related to the Mortellis." Tristan leaned over and picked up a stick and tossed it into the pit.

"That's what we call burying the lead," she mumbled. "So, my parents didn't just one day decide to become criminals." She rubbed her temples. No amount of tequila was going to drown out that little piece of information.

"My whole life is a lie." Lizzy stood in front of the window in her bedroom and stared at the water. Moving back to Lake George had been both a blessing and a curse. She'd found a sense of duty and honor here that she hadn't found anywhere else.

And Station 29 had become her home.

Morgan slipped his arms around her middle and rested his chin on her shoulder. "No. Don't think that way."

She leaned into him and closed her eyes, sucking up as much of his strength as possible. "Are your parents mad?" she asked, opting to change the subject.

"Why would they be? I'm a grown man. I can come and go as I please. I don't have to tell them I'm staying the night somewhere else." His words were filled with a lightness that she so desperately needed.

"You know what I meant."

"They are just glad that I told them I was in town, and they didn't have to find out by driving by when they went out in the morning."

"You don't have to stay with me tonight if you don't want to."

He laughed. "Yeah, but if I don't, you'll call and ask me to watch you fall asleep. I might as well do that in person." He kissed the sensitive spot under her ear. "It's late and your alarm is going off at four thirty in the morning. Let's get some sleep." He tugged her toward the bed, pulling back the sheets. He wore nothing but his boxers, which hung low on his hips.

The light of the moon caught his dark hair, and he'd grown a bit of a beard and mustache over the course of the last few weeks. She reached out and touched his face. "Why do I even like you?"

"I don't know. I don't like myself half the time." He turned off the lights and slipped under the covers.

She lay on her side with her hands tucked under her cheek, staring.

"What?"

"You're a good man," she whispered. "I don't know what I would have done without you."

He brushed her hair over her shoulder. "You would have survived. You've got a lot of people in this town who care about you."

"You make me want to change my mind about a lot of things," she whispered. Now was not the time for confessions. He would go back to his mountain and eventually move on to another lady. That was what he did. And she, of all people, should be okay with it.

But she wasn't.

She wanted to explore things with Morgan, but she shouldn't even go there. It would be too awkward in the long run.

"Like what?"

"Nothing. I don't know what I'm talking about. Too much tequila."

"You barely had any." He rested his hand on her hip. His thumb rubbed a tender circle on her bare skin just above the fabric of her panties. "What's on your mind?"

"You," she whispered.

"You've been on my mind for a long while now." He smiled. "I just didn't think your nightclubbing and dancing would go with the stars in my sky."

"I think that's called a disco ball."

He laughed. "That's a good one, but let's not doctor this up with humor and avoid what you want to talk about."

"And what is it that you think I want to discuss?"

"Us," he said. "I don't drive down from the Dix Range for just anyone on a whim."

"I see."

"I don't think you do." He traced a path up her side with his index finger, tugging at the fabric of her nightshirt. "We've both had our reasons for not wanting to be in a committed relationship, but you've made me realize I am lonely."

Her pulse picked up a notch, and her lungs deflated. This both excited her and broke her heart. "I don't want you to feel that way."

"I never did until you moved here, and now I go back to my home, and it feels empty. Like something or someone is missing."

"Wow. That's heavy."

"I know. And it scares the crap out of me for more than one reason." He leaned in and brushed his lips over his in a sweet and tender kiss. Her skin warmed as if she'd been wrapped in a heated blanket and placed in front of a crackling fire.

"I'm falling for you, Lizzy Cohen, and I don't know what to do about that except let it happen."

She gasped. Fighting tears, she blinked. She had already fallen for him, but she couldn't bring herself to say the words out loud or even silently to herself. But she no longer wanted to find a job somewhere else. She wanted to stay right at Station 29.

But even that meant a long-distance relationship, though it was better than nothing.

"What are you thinking?" he asked.

"I might be thinking that I want to give this a try."

Before she knew what happened, he'd removed her nightshirt, and his hands cupped her breasts, massaging gently, while his tongue was dancing with hers in a wild dance that only he could perform.

He had a way of making her feel as though no

one else mattered. That she was his entire world and that he would walk on water if it were necessary.

The way he kissed set her blood on fire and curled her toes. No man had ever made her feel this way, and she suspected no one would compare to Morgan.

She loved him. There was no doubt about that. Somehow he managed to wiggle his way into her heart and she never wanted to let go.

Pushing him to his back, she removed his boxers and took him into her mouth with the kind of passion she hoped he'd never forget. It was as if she were leaving her mark on him so any woman after her would know she'd been there first, and he'd cared enough to come down from his mountain and give her a try.

"Hey," he said, tugging at her hair.

She glanced up, holding him tightly, squeezing and stroking. She needed to please him and when he batted her hands away, she frowned. "What's wrong?"

"I was going to ask you the same thing." He pulled her to his chest, gently rolling her over. "You seem desperate."

"What does that mean?" She sucked in a deep breath, but it was between his weight on her and the utter terror of him not falling as hard for her as she'd done for him.

"It means that while I love everything you were doing, I didn't want the night to end like that." He nuzzled himself between her legs, entering her in one long, powerful thrust. "I'd rather it end like this."

She arched into him, digging her nails into his back. Fireworks went off inside her head. Her body immediately responded to him so intently she thought she might scream. It was as if every inch of her burned so hot she ignited into flames, and yet it felt so good.

"Yes," she said with a throaty moan. No man had ever loved her the way Morgan did. "Please. I need you."

He fanned her face, running his thumbs across her cheeks, staring into her eyes with his blue orbs. He kissed her nose, stroking her insides slowly, building up the pressure until it was unbearable.

She grinded against him, begging for release.

And he gave her exactly what she demanded.

"Oh, my God. Morgan. Yes." A slow tickle started at her toes and crawled up her body. She shivered and it built more intense until she convulsed, jerking wildly with her orgasm.

He slammed into her three times before his

climax tore into her like a sailboat keeling in a strong wind. He nuzzled his face in her neck, kissing her tenderly and whispering sweet nothings in her ear.

It was in that moment she knew she'd never want another man.

Ever.

9

*L*izzy took a deep breath and let it out slowly. She held the piece of paper with her well-rehearsed speech with a death grip.

"Relax," Morgan whispered as he took her into his arms.

She dropped her head onto his strong shoulders. He'd been such a rock in her life since this whole shitshow began. "Any news from Tristan or his buddies?"

"Actually, Tristan's wife is in labor. However, Jake is working on it. But this hearing is pretty long and if he's got something, he'll be here. Otherwise, he'll be a no-show."

"I just hope he has better luck deciphering all those letters than we did."

The door to the courtroom opened. A man peeked his head outside. "We're ready for you, Miss. Cohen."

"Hey. Just remember, even though I can't be there with you…" Morgan paused. "Oh, fuck it. Not the place I wanted to say this and it's certainly not very romantic, but know that I love you. Crazy as it sounds and coming from me of all people, but it's true. I love you."

Lizzy blinked. Her heart swelled. Tears formed in the corners of her eyes. To hear those words now meant more to her than if he'd said them over the most romantic candlelight dinner with a big bottle of tequila and roses. She palmed his freshly shaven face. "You are the sweetest man I've ever met, and what's even crazier is that I love you back."

He kissed her in a passionate but quick kiss. "No matter what happens, you did the right thing."

She nodded, squeezing his hand as she approached the doors. She didn't let go until she stepped between them.

No sooner did she enter the courtroom than the doors slammed shut. She glanced over her shoulder, but Morgan was no longer in her sight.

But he was in her heart.

He loved her.

And she loved him.

That was something her parents couldn't take from her. It was private and something they knew nothing about. As a matter of fact, her parents had no power over her at all anymore.

A great weight had been lifted from her shoulders.

She eased down the center of the room. Her parents turned their heads and smiled.

She did not return the sentiment.

"Miss Cohen," the judge said, "I understand you'd like to speak to the court about whether or not your parents should be granted early parole."

"Yes, Your Honor." She went to the podium and flattened out her paper. She glanced once at her parents, catching her mother's scrutinizing gaze.

It was not that of a mom who adored her daughter.

But of one who wanted something.

A look she'd seen often but didn't understand as a kid.

Well, she did now.

"Please proceed," the judge said.

"Thank you." Lizzy cleared her throat. "I realize I

was just a kid when my parents committed their crimes, and at the time, I was scared and confused. I'd lost my entire world. My best friend had died sleeping right next to me. My parents had been arrested. I didn't understand much of what was happening around me. However, as time passed and I grew into an adult, I've come to understand a few things. But there is one thing that I cannot let go of and that is the fact that my parents had my cell phone which had a text from Karen Land that clearly stated not to come over, that I was sneaking out of the house and going to her place."

"If you don't mind me intruding," the judge said.

"Not at all." Of course she did because to her, that felt like the judge was going to side with her parents for some reason. It made her nervous in general, but what was she going to do, argue with the judge?

"I've read the transcripts from the trial, and that evidence was not allowed during proceedings. And furthermore, I have a teenage daughter and getting her to let me see what is on her phone is like pulling teeth. She constantly changes her password on me."

"I did the same thing, but I found out once living at my aunt's that my parents had installed a program on my computer where they could see everything, including my passwords. They would have had access."

"And you believe they would have seen that text that night and set that fire knowing you were there?" the judge said.

"I would never!" Her mother stood, knocking over her chair.

"Order in my courtroom," the judge said.

"I'm saying that they had access to my text messages because they were in possession of my cell. I've recently learned that they used my cell to make calls that night."

"Your Honor," her parents' attorney said. "That was all inadmissible and this is supposed to just be a statement, not a witch hunt."

"I agree," the judge said. "You don't want your parents to be paroled, do you?"

"No, sir," she said with a thick frog in her throat.

"Why not?"

"I only have my memories to base this on, and I was just a kid, but I believe my parents are responsible for at least a dozen other fires."

"Your Honor. Please. This is a parole hearing, not a trial," the attorney said.

"I'm sorry, Your Honor, but I fear for my life if

they are released. I was in that house. I believe they knew I was there."

The man who called her into the courtroom waltzed over to the judge and handed him a note. The judge unfolded it and cocked his head.

Not a great poker face, but Lizzy didn't know if that was good or bad.

"I'm sorry about the interruption. Miss Cohen, would you mind taking a seat."

"No, sir." Lizzy made herself as comfortable as possible on the front bench opposite her parents, doing her best not to look at them. It freaked her out how much she resembled her mother.

The doors to the courtroom opened, and Lizzy glanced over her shoulder to see Jared and Jake stroll into the room, dressed up in their trooper uniforms and looking all official.

Jared walked right up to the judge's podium and handed him a piece of paper. The judge looked it over and nodded. "Thank you, Sergeant. I guess my role here is done."

Jared turned and handed the piece of paper to her parents' attorney.

"What is the meaning of this?" the attorney asked. "Oh no. You can't do this."

"I just did," Jared said.

Her father snatched the paper. "This is bullshit. These are trumped-up charges. We will fight these and win, and then have your badge."

"Better people than you have tried to get it, so have fun with that." Jared nodded his head once.

"What is going on?" she asked Jake.

"We found the smoking gun on the other fires and that is a warrant for their arrest. They won't be paroled today, and sadly, they are facing new charges with up to maybe another twenty-five years or so in prison."

"Seriously?"

Jake nodded. "Tristan was able to decipher some things in those letters. We found the money, and along with some good detective work, we were able to find some new evidence. Now, it's not over—"

"It's over enough." She took off running. She needed to see Morgan, and she didn't have to go too far, as he met her at the door. "Did you hear?" She leaped up into his arms, wrapping her legs around his body.

He stumbled backward, nearly taking out three people before hitting his back on the wall.

He groaned. "I did. Sounds like you just got a nice birthday present."

She cupped his cheeks. "The only birthday

present I want is you out on that dance floor." She arched a brow. "Or did you forget you made that promise?"

"Nope. I didn't. But then you're coming to my mountain."

"I'm still taking that week off, so you'll be stuck with me."

"I hope I will be stuck with you for a lot longer than a week."

10

---

*M*organ spent the entire day cleaning, and now he was totally freaked out because he'd made a fucking mess of the kitchen. All he wanted to do was impress Lizzy with his mad cooking skills.

Which he didn't possess.

But he wanted to try.

He pulled the pie out of the oven. It looked like shit, but it smelled scrumptious. That was at least a good sign.

He lifted the top of the skillet and filled the wooden spoon with pasta and cream sauce, making sure he got a little piece of the meat.

Not bad if he did say so himself.

The smell of something burning caught his

attention. He glanced around the kitchen, but there was nothing that could possibly create that scent. As a matter of fact, it smelled more like burning wood.

He glanced toward the family room and out the big picture window. He dropped the spoon onto the hardwood floors. "Fuck." He reached for his cell. The flames from the brush fire reached for the sky like fingers dancing. The fire appeared to flank on the east and south sides of his house, and on the far side of the road.

He pulled up Lizzy's number. It went right to voicemail. Shit.

His next call was to first responders.

"This is 9-1-1, what's your emergency?"

"I want to report a brush fire on Old Rank Road about three miles in, close to the dead end and up the hill about a half a mile." He stepped outside and gasped. "It's surrounding my home."

"Sir, where exactly are you?"

"In my house at 18901 Old Rank Road, the fire is spreading quickly." He raced to his shed and hooked up the hoses, turning them on, letting them go wild. Any amount of water would help. Next stop would be the sprinkler system that he rarely used. He inhaled sharply, smelling gas.

That wasn't good.

"My name is Morgan Farren. I'm a ranger for the Dix Range. I'm going to hang up and call my boss."

"Sir, that's not—"

"I know the protocol, but I need to make some calls while I try to save my home."

"You need to evacuate—"

He tapped his cell. The only way he was getting out at this point was driving through the flames, which wasn't a bad idea. That was until he entered his garage and found all three vehicles had the tires slashed.

Fuck.

He tapped Tristan's number who picked up on the first ring. "What's up, man?"

"I'm in trouble. Big trouble."

"Love does that to a man."

"Not that kind. I'm standing in the middle of a circle fire that was obviously started intentionally, and I've got no way of getting out. I've called 9-1-1. I know the firefighters up here are on the way, but this was no accident and I'd bet my bottom dollar I know who had it started."

"I'll call Jared. He'll get the ball rolling."

"Lizzy was supposed to be here, but she's not answering her phone."

"Jesus. Okay. Keep trying her and hang tight."

"I have about maybe forty minutes before this fire reaches the house. I've got some resources, but not many."

The sound of a chopper overhead eased his mind just a little. But not much. He made his way toward the detached storage garage, where he kept his snowmobiles and ATVs. Hopefully whoever had slashed his tires hadn't gotten to those. He reached the key code lock and noticed the door was ajar.

Slowly, he pulled back the door.

Shit. His heart sank when he saw Lizzy sitting in the center, tied to a chair, her head drooping, obviously unconscious.

"Nice of you to join us."

"Who the fuck are you?"

"No one who matters," the man holding the gun said.

"Obviously, since this place is about to become kindling and you're going to die with me."

"Oh. I'll make it out alive. But you won't, and you've just made my life a whole lot easier. Now come over here and sit." He waved his gun to the bench he had Lizzy tied to.

Morgan glanced around, wishing he'd been smart enough to take his gun with him, but he'd been more concerned about getting the water system going than intruders. He rolled his neck. He had a few options, but he had to get to them first and that might be hard if he ended up with his hands behind his back.

"I'm curious," Morgan said as he leaned over, checking on Lizzy.

Her chest rose up and down, so that was good.

He reached out to brush her hair from her face, but the man with the gun smacked his arm away.

"She's alive and fine. Now what the fuck are you curious about?"

"A couple of things. How do you plan on getting out alive? I can feel the heat from that fire, and it's going to take this building down in minutes. And secondly, and maybe more importantly, who do you work for?"

"I think you know the answer to the second question."

"Mortelli."

"Now look at you growing a brain," the man with the gun said.

"Perhaps. However, I still can't figure out how you're getting out of here when that fire isn't going to allow you to walk through it."

"My boss is sending a chopper in for me."

"I don't hear anything but the roar of flames, and

it's getting closer and closer. If I were you, I'd check on that boss of yours. Maybe you're collateral damage after all."

The man with the gun parted his lips, and for a brief moment, it looked as though he might question if someone was coming for him or not. "Sit your ass down," he said.

Morgan had about enough of this, and there was no way he was going to let this asshole tie him up. He did, however, lower himself as if he were going to sit. He just needed to position himself a certain way when he noticed slight movement from Lizzy.

He leaned lower. She tilted her head and she actually winked.

Well, hot fucking damn.

"You know what," Morgan said. "I don't think this is working out for me."

"What?" The man with the gun lowered his arm just enough that Morgan felt comfortable bolting upright.

He knocked the gun out of the man's hand, and immediately sucker punched him in the gut and then kneed him in the face before kicking him to the ground. Morgan lifted him to his feet and took the rope, securing his hands before attending to Lizzy.

"I thought you'd never get your ass out here."

"It's nice to see you too," he said. "But we've got a bigger problem than this asshole and whoever is coming to get him."

"I can see that," she said.

He pulled out his cell and brought up the ranger station.

"You're both going to die," the man, now without the gun, said. "My boss is going to kill you."

"You just need to shut up," Morgan said, shoving the man into the seat. He found some tape and put it over the man's mouth.

"What are you doing?" Lizzy asked.

"What I should have done to begin with."

"This is Lieutenant Arnold."

"Hey, this is Morgan."

"Jesus. I heard there's a fire up by you. They sent three crews. They aren't there yet?"

"I hear the sirens, but I need a chopper to get me, my girlfriend, and the asshat who set the fucking fire out of here, but I also need you to call my buddy Jared at the Troop G office of the NY State Troopers and have them try to find a private chopper in the area. It's one of Mortelli's men."

"Who?"

"Just tell Jared that. He'll know what it means.

Now get someone to me ASAP because we don't have much time."

"On it if I have to go out there myself," Arnold said.

"Send me a text if you hear anything about the bad guy's helicopter."

"Will do," Arnold said.

Just to be safe, Morgan sent a message to Jared.

"I want to go outside and see what this fire is doing," Lizzy said.

"I'm going with you, and we should bring this guy with us." Morgan snagged the gun, checked the safety, and secured it in his pants. He yanked the bad guy from his seat and followed Lizzy out the door. He immediately was assaulted with the wild scent of burning wood, pine, and leaves. The hair on his arms stood on end as the heat from the flames only a good fifty feet away from his home now threatened to overtake everything in its path, including him and Lizzy.

"My God," Lizzy whispered. "What the hell kind of accelerant did they use?" She grabbed his cell. "I was only in there for a half hour, and it was down by the road."

The *whop whop* of a helicopter overhead caught

his attention. He glanced up and smiled. "That's a state trooper chopper."

A ladder dropped from the opening as the aircraft lowered.

"I hope they can save your home," Lizzy said. "I really like it up here."

He helped one of the troopers with the criminal, hoisting him on the harness. "I can replace things. I can't replace people." He took her into his arms. "I'd die if anything ever happened to you."

"I'd be lost without you." She took ahold of the ladder and started climbing toward safety.

"Good to know," he said, following her into the chopper.

They might have gotten caught in the flames, but he'd follow her anywhere.

Lizzy stretched out her legs and leaned back in the metal chair. "These are god-awful."

Morgan squeezed her thigh. "Better than being in the center of a fire."

"That's not funny." She twisted her hair into a bun on top of her head. "Have you heard anything about your house?"

"So far, they've kept the fire from touching it."

"It's not out yet?" It had been a dry summer, and that meant the trees were ripe to burn, as well as the grass and everything else in the path of those flames. When you add in the gas accelerant, she wasn't surprised that it was taking a while to not just contain the fire, but put it out.

"Last I heard from Arnold, it was close," Morgan said.

"I'm so sorry."

He furrowed his brow. "For what?"

"I brought all this to your front door."

He took her chin with his thumb and forefinger. "You did no such thing." He brushed his lips over hers in a tender kiss.

Her life had taken a turn she hadn't been prepared for and she still wasn't sure how to deal with it. Morgan came out of nowhere, as did her love for him.

Someone cleared their throat.

She blinked, breaking off the kiss.

"Sorry to interrupt," Jared said. "I thought you might like to know that we have tracked down and arrested the man who was to pick up your captor in the helicopter."

"That makes me feel a lot better." Morgan stood. "But what about Mortelli and his gang?"

"Do I need to be looking over my shoulder for the rest of my life?" Lizzy asked as she pushed herself from her chair. Her body ached and her wrists burned from where they'd been tied up.

"The good news is that neither of those men were hired by Mortelli," Jared said.

"How can you be sure?" Morgan looped his arm around her shoulders in a protective wrap.

"The Feds came in and questioned them, and between not being on the Feds' radar and saying bullshit things about the operation, acting as if they were badass, we all came to the conclusion these two goons were copycat wannabes. But more importantly, the Mortellis have pulled out of the area, and according to the Feds, they have a guy deep undercover who has confirmed that Mortelli didn't give this order and these aren't his people and that your parents are dead to them."

Lizzy shivered. "I'm not sure what to do with that statement."

Jared reached out and squeezed her shoulder. "Live your life."

"That's good advice." She glanced up at Morgan. "And I want to live it right here."

"If she goes into a full-out wail, she's all yours for the night."

"Deal."

"So, how's the move going?" Stanley, Morgan's father, asked. "I still can't believe you sold that house *and* gave up being a ranger."

"I didn't give up anything, Dad." Morgan raised his wine glass and took a long sip. "I'm just transferring my skills to being a trooper."

"And moving back to Lake George, where you belong," Edna, his mother, said with a beaming smile.

Morgan laughed. "You're just happy that I bought a house on Cleverdale, only a few blocks away from you."

"No. I'm ecstatic that you finally found a woman that completes you."

Lizzy's cheeks heated. The one thing they hadn't told them was that she was moving in with Morgan. And while it didn't matter because they were grown-ups and could do what they wanted, she knew his parents wanted a wedding, but kudos to them for not constantly bringing it up and putting pressure on them. She struggled with all the changes as it was and sometimes worried that Morgan was making too many adjustments to his life and she wasn't making any.

However, she hadn't asked him to make a single one, and every time he suggested he make a major change, he didn't just do it; he brought her into the mix, discussed it with her, and explained why he wanted to do it.

Loving him was so easy, and sometimes that scared her, but it wasn't enough for her to run away.

And he didn't want to go back to hiding out in any mountain range. He was ready to start living his life in civilization.

And she was ready to share hers.

"I am too," Morgan said, taking her hand.

Andrea's cries grew louder in the background.

"And before my beautiful niece ruins this with her inability to sleep somewhere else, I might as well get this over with." He stood and reached deep into his pocket, pulling out a velvet pouch.

The air in Lizzy's lungs escaped in a big swish. She clutched her chest. "No," she whispered.

"I really hope that's not going to be your answer." He bent on one knee. "I love you, Lizzy, and I want to spend the rest of my life showing you just how much. Will you marry me?"

She glanced down at the diamond ring sparkling

like the brightest star in the night sky. "Seriously?" She lifted her gaze. "That's for me?"

"No one else makes my heart beat a little faster."

"Oh, my God," she whispered. "I can't believe you're doing this."

"Me neither," he said. "Are you going to answer me, or are you going to leave me hanging?"

"Yes. A million times, yes." She wiggled her hand.

He placed the ring on her finger before taking her into his arms.

"Well, this calls for a big celebration," Stanley said. "Let's break out the bubbly."

"Spencer, get that daughter of ours out of that pack 'n play," Echo said. "We're just going to have to deal."

"Yes, dear." Spencer tossed his napkin to the table and smiled.

"I never thought I'd see this day," Edna said, swiping at her face.

"Mom. Don't start crying." Morgan took his mother in his arms and hugged her.

"I can't help it." She pushed him aside and took Lizzy by the hands. "Thank you for bringing my son to his senses."

"I think it was the other way around."

"I don't care how it was. I'm just so happy for both of you. Now, make me more grandbabies."

"Mom. We don't even have a date set, much less had that conversation."

"Come on, dear, let's go get some champagne and let these two lovebirds have a few moments alone." Stanley took Edna by the elbow and led her toward the kitchen.

Echo and Spencer had disappeared upstairs, leaving her and Morgan all alone.

"Wow, that was a surprise," she whispered as Morgan took her into his arms, kissing her cheek.

"I hope in a good way. I wasn't sure if you'd be okay with me doing that in front of my family, but it just felt right."

"It was perfect." She tilted her head and stared into his beautiful loving blue eyes. "I do want to have children. Is that something you can get on board with?"

"We can start working on that part of our lives tonight, if you'd like."

She laughed. "Oh, and about that wedding. I don't want a big deal. I don't need the white dress, the church, or any of that."

"What about right here at my parents' house in a couple of weeks."

"Sounds perfect."

"I love you, Lizzy." He kissed her tenderly.

If there was any man she would ever consider getting caught in the flames with, it would be Morgan.

Thank you for reading *Caught in the Flames.* Please feel free to leave an honest review. Next up is:
Chasing The Fire

If you want to learn more about Jared and his story, check out: ***In Two Weeks***
And for more information about Tristen and Brook please check out: ***When A Stranger Calls***
And here is Jake Prichard's story: ***To Protect His own***

Grab a glass of vino, kick back, relax, and let the romance roll in…

Sign up for my Newsletter (https://dl.bookfunnel.com/ 82gm8b9k4y) where I often give away free books before publication.

Join my private Facebook group (https://www.facebook.

com/groups/191706547909047/) where I post exclusive excerpts and discuss all things murder and love!

ABOUT THE AUTHOR

Jen Talty is the *USA Today* Bestselling Author of Contemporary Romance, Romantic Suspense, and Paranormal Romance. In the fall of 2020, her short story was selected and featured in a 1001 Dark Nights Anthology.

Regardless of the genre, her goal is to take you on a ride that will leave you floating under the sun with warmth in your heart. She writes stories about broken heroes and heroines who aren't necessarily looking for romance, but in the end, they find the kind of love books are written about :).

She first started writing while carting her kids to one hockey rink after the other, averaging 170 games per year between 3 kids in 2 countries and 5 states. Her first book, IN TWO WEEKS was originally published in 2007. In 2010 she helped form a publishing company (Cool Gus Publishing) with *NY Times* Bestselling Author Bob Mayer where she ran the technical side of the business through 2016.

Jen is currently enjoying the next phase of her life… the empty nester! She and her husband reside in Jupiter, Florida.

Grab a glass of vino, kick back, relax, and let the romance roll in…

Sign up for my Newsletter (https://dl.bookfunnel. com/82gm8b9k4y) where I often give away free books before publication.

Join my private Facebook group (https://www.facebook. com/groups/191706547909047/) where I post exclusive excerpts and discuss all things murder and love!

Never miss a new release. Follow me on Amazon:amazon.com/author/jentalty

And on Bookbub: bookbub.com/authors/jen-talty

ALSO BY JEN TALTY

Brand new series: SAFE HARBOR!

Mine To Keep

Mine To Save

Mine To Protect

Mine to Hold

Mine to Love

Check out LOVE IN THE ADIRONDACKS!

Shattered Dreams

An Inconvenient Flame

The Wedding Driver

Clear Blue Sky

Blue Moon

Before the Storm

NY STATE TROOPER SERIES (also set in the Adirondacks!)

In Two Weeks

Dark Water

Deadly Secrets

Jack Daniels

Jim Beam

Whiskey Sour

Whiskey Cobbler

Whiskey Smash

Irish Whiskey

The Monroes

Color Me Yours

Color Me Smart

Color Me Free

Color Me Lucky

Color Me Ice

Color Me Home

Search and Rescue

Protecting Ainsley

Protecting Clover

Protecting Olympia

Protecting Freedom

Protecting Princess

Protecting Marlowe

Fallport Rescue Operations

The Matriarch

Aegis Network: Jacksonville Division

A SEAL's Honor

Talon's Honor

Arthur's Honor

Rex's Honor

Kent's Honor

Aegis Network Short Stories

Max & Milian

A Christmas Miracle

Spinning Wheels

Holiday's Vacation

The Brotherhood Protectors

Out of the Wild

Rough Justice

Rough Around The Edges

Rough Ride

Rough Edge

Rough Beauty

The Brotherhood Protectors

The Saving Series